Emma's Luck

Emma's Luck

CLAUDIA SCHREIBER

Translated from the German
by Anthea Bell

JOHN MURRAY

First published in Great Britain in 2008 by John Murray (Publishers)
An Hachette Livre UK company

I

© Claudia Schreiber 2003
Translation © Anthea Bell 2008

The translation of this work was supported by a grant from the Goethe-Institut,
which is funded by the German Ministry of Foreign Affairs.

A CIP catalogue record for this title is available from the British Library

ISBN 978-0-7195-2091-4

Typeset in Garamond MT by
Palimpsest Book Production Limited, Grangemouth, Stirlingshire

Printed and bound by Clays Ltd, St Ives plc

John Murray policy is to use papers that are natural, renewable and
recyclable products and made from wood grown in sustainable forests.
The logging and manufacturing processes are expected to conform to the
environmental regulations of the country of origin.

John Murray (Publishers)
338 Euston Road
London NW1 3BH

www.johnmurray.co.uk

For Helmut

Emma, did my love for you
Make me foolish, or was love
Sure to spring from my mad folly?
Emma, Emma, tell me true.

I'm tormented, dearest Emma
Not by mere infatuation,
Not just by my lovesick madness,
But by this abstruse dilemma.

Heinrich Heine

*E*mma's bedroom was a pigsty. Underwear spilled out of drawers and the wardrobe; piles of old newspapers and unpaid bills had grown into a bedside table and a stool; fist-sized balls of dust-fluff danced about under the bed, stopping when they came up against the remnants of half-eaten sandwiches.

Outside, the rising sun was painting the fields red, and dew fell on the grass. Emma wrapped herself tightly in her quilt and snuggled into it. She envied her pigs, lying out there side by side on the fresh straw, breathing in time with each other. Their days were so deliciously full of doing nothing. Early or late, day or night – they just lounged around the place, they wallowed, they fed, they scraped their backs pleasurably against the garden fence, and they lay down nestling close together. And when this enviable life had given them a nice layer of fat, Emma provided them with a beautiful end: quick and painless. The whole meaning of their piggy life was then made manifest in heavenly sausages.

No life on earth seemed to Emma simpler, more delightful, more meaningful and fulfilled than the life of a pig on her own farm.

*

She got up and went outside barefoot, in her tatty old nightie. The rooster stalked proudly up to meet her, like the farm's commanding officer on duty. Emma saluted, and in reply he appeared to announce punctiliously, 'Nothing special to report. Farm and farmhouse all in order.' The cat rubbed around her legs, asking to be petted, and followed her into the garden.

There were flowers everywhere, and good strong plants lined the wooden fence. Courgettes, peppers, leeks, tomatoes – they were all flourishing, nothing had been eaten by slugs or attacked by aphids. Emma picked a few raspberries and popped them into her mouth. She liked to feel the warmth of the damp ground under her bare feet. Contentedly, she breathed in the summer air and looked up at a lark singing in the air just above her.

In the cowshed, she said good morning to her cow with a hefty slap on the back. She lay down under the cow's belly and milked the udder straight into her mouth to quench her morning thirst. The jet didn't always go the right way; milk splashed into her eyes, on to her throat, trickled down the neck of her nightie. Emma wiped her mouth on her forearm like a child, blissfully satisfied. Then she went into the hen house and collected three eggs.

She switched on breakfast television in the kitchen, as she did every morning, and put a pan on the stove. Her favourite presenter was on screen. He said, 'Good morning, viewers.' But on her own TV set, Emma clearly heard his affectionate and very personal, 'Good morning, Emma.' She said good morning back, then turned away, smiling, fried the eggs and cut some bread.

At that moment a car drew up outside. From the familiar sound of it Emma identified Henner's old police car, a VW Beetle. Emma wiped a peephole in her dirty windowpane to see if the village policeman was or wasn't wearing his cap. Without his cap he came with peaceful intentions, with his cap he came to make a nuisance of himself.

Henner had his cap on!

Cursing, Emma reached for the loaded shotgun that always stood beside her stove and went out, barefoot, in her milk-stained nightie and her knickers.

Henner was standing beside his green-and-white car holding a large envelope. He knew he had very bad news for Emma, and he knew Emma knew it too, so he forgave her for marching towards him with a loaded gun, shouting, 'You get out of my farm this minute, you pen-pushing old fart!'

Poor Henner was caught between two fronts. A fearsome screeching rose into the air behind him. His mother had come along too. She was forcing her gigantic bottom out of the Beetle backwards, and while still wedged between the seat and the door she was already shouting angrily at Emma.

'I'll have you know my Henner's here in the line of duty. He can bring charges, he can have you jailed for vulgar abuse, so he can, for insulting an officer of the law!'

Only now did the old woman stand upright, emerging from a grey cloud of tobacco smoke. The stub of a cigarette she had rolled for herself clung to the slack corner of her mouth. Spit was running out of the corner of her mouth too. She sucked the nicotine out of the cigarette stub, closed her old eyes because the smoke irritated the mucous membrane, and said, with a scornful glance at Emma's dirty nightie, 'And what do you think *that* looks like?'

By *that* she meant not the nightie but Emma personally. Women were regarded as neuter beings in these parts.

Emma was almost bursting with fury. She fired helplessly into the air. Evidently that was nothing new to Henner. He didn't even move a muscle, he just looked sad, like a dog with sore eyes, and begged his mother, 'Get back in the car, or I'm never taking you out with me again.' And he asked Emma, 'Please, don't make this even harder for me.'

In silence, he indicated the envelope he was holding.

'The deadline's three months tomorrow. You have to be out by then. You can't take the animals, they'll go into the auction.'

Emma raised her fist as if it held a knife. 'I'll give you auction! If anyone comes and tries to take the farm away from me, I'll stick him like a pig, I swear I will.'

Henner knew she'd do it, too. This was a woman used to killing. He wagged his forefinger feebly at her.

'I didn't hear that, Emma.'

Now she was aiming the barrel of the gun right at his flies.

'You get out of here, Henner, or I'll shoot it off.'

Henner ventured a timid smile and looked at her wet nightie. Her bare breasts were outlined beneath it. Resigned, he took off his uniform cap and made her yet another proposal of marriage. His wording was unlikely to succeed with anyone but Emma.

'Move in with me, why don't you, you silly cow?'

Emma lowered her gun. A faint smile played around the corners of her mouth. Henner had touched her heart.

4

Fat little Henner! Small and ugly as he was, timorous and weak, he was still the only man who had ever wanted her. The first time he'd been all of seven years old, and she'd been six.

Neither of them had much idea what to do. All the same, he went off with her to the maize field, where the whole village did it. Maize was grown in these parts solely for that purpose.

She took her knickers off, lay down between two rows of the tall plants, and spread her legs. Henner looked and . . . did nothing.

'You have to put your thingy in now, Henner,' said Emma helpfully.

In where? they both wondered, and neither of them let the other see how little they knew about it. Henner took his trousers down. There it hung, small as a radish and so round. So red too! Emma picked a young corn cob, stripped off the husks until a cob of about the right size was left. She handed it to him. Young Henner nudged Emma's behind with the corn cob, and that was it.

Both of them pulled up their clothes again. Emma stuck her tongue out at Henner and walked away.

They grew up. His little radish didn't, though, it stayed round and red. But Emma was finally deflowered after all, with a ripe corn cob manually guided by Henner.

The two of them were fond of each other. They'd known each other intimately for many years, but Emma would never want to marry Henner.

Suppose she lost her farm, though? That did make a difference. If only it hadn't been for that mother of his, always at his side, unable to share him with anyone, still wiping his face with her spit on a hanky, no shame about it at all, and he didn't even dare resist that!

With a glance at the old lady, who was back sitting in the car and had lit another cigarette, Emma told Henner, in composed tones, 'You can have me if *she* goes.'

Henner began stammering. Emma knew what that meant at once.

Her face darkened. The expression at the corners of her mouth grew hard again. She raised the gun and fired at the ground right beside his feet without warning, once to the right and once to the left.

Henner shook his head sadly, and put the papers he was holding down on the bloodstained block of wood where Emma cut the chickens' heads off. Without another word, he got into his rickety VW and drove away from the farm.

'You're not a man, you little radish, you!' Emma shouted after him. 'A man living with his mummy at your age . . . whoever heard of such a thing?'

But as soon as the car had disappeared beyond the hills, Emma's mouth twisted and tears flowed down her cheeks. She gave the large envelope a cursory glance. She wasn't going to open it, she wasn't going to read the contents, she didn't want to know what it told her in its bureaucratic jargon.

Emma groaned as if that would sweep all her worries out of her mind. She hadn't paid any bills for two years. The price of livestock had fallen. She could rear and kill as many pigs as she liked, but what had provided for whole generations on this farm in the past wasn't enough now even for Emma herself.

6

A piglet made its way up to her and nuzzled her leg. Emma crouched down and took it in her arms. Pressed her face into the soft bristles, and went back into her house with the piglet in her arms.

*M*ax tossed and turned in bed, tormented once again by his dreams: an open bottle of red wine was tipping over in slow motion to spill its contents on his dazzlingly white carpet. He tried to catch it, but grasped only empty air. He kept on and on grasping empty air, and at this point he always woke up. Screaming. Because the red wine had ruined the carpet. He never managed to catch that bottle. And always, just as it fell right over, he woke up in terror.

His books were systematically arranged on the shelves. Unread. He borrowed the books he read. He didn't touch his own, he was keeping them just in case the municipal library closed down. The idea that there might be no books left that he hadn't read scared him. Everything that could come to an end scared Max. And it wasn't just the books. Almost everything in this life, almost everything on earth could end. The water supply, for instance. So Max went easy on the water, washing himself in the bathroom basin with a flannel. The municipal water authority had already changed his water meter twice because his low use of water had aroused their suspicions. When he got up in the morning Max used exactly the same amount of water for washing as he did in the coffee machine.

9

He ate breakfast on weekdays at six-thirty, and at the weekend an hour later by candlelight and to the accompaniment of classical music, the table laid like something in a five-star hotel, with a damask napkin that he hardly soiled at all.

That had been his parents' custom, celebrating the ritual of this little luxury, and thus reminding themselves daily how lucky they were that it wasn't wartime now, and they weren't starving. There was never muesli without Mozart, there was no Vivaldi without an egg. So from early childhood Max had been familiar with cantatas, preludes and symphonies . . . anything as long as it wasn't atonal.

He had a set breakfast menu: on Mondays, Wednesdays and Fridays he ate wholemeal bread with curd cheese and fresh cress, on Tuesdays and Thursdays he had oatflakes with plain yoghurt. On Saturday he ate scrambled eggs and bacon, on Sunday it was fresh fruit salad. He kept strictly to this menu. It made life easier for him.

After breakfast Max immediately washed the few dishes he had used, dried them and put them back in the cupboard. He pushed the only chair in the kitchen back under the table, taking care that it was at a right angle to the edge of the table itself. After Max had closed the front door, he breathed on the door handle and polished it with the sleeve of his coat. The shiny brass made him feel happy.

Max walked down a shopping street, past boutiques, a butcher's, and finally an electrical goods store with ten TV sets in the shop window, all flickering away on various channels. He was on his way to see the doctor; he had already pressed the doorbell of the surgery, which was next door to the electrical goods store. It was some time before the door opened, and meanwhile Max looked at the TV sets on display. They all showed a breakfast news presenter. Max shook his head. How could anyone talk so much so early in the morning? And who watched TV so early anyway?

He turned away, looked at the pedestrians, and his glance fell on the other side of the street. There was a beer garden there. The garden chairs were standing untidily all over the place; some had even fallen over. The place was in total disorder. The sight of it upset Max. At last the door-opener of the surgery buzzed.

Dr Deckstein liked to work standing up, so as not to spoil the creases in his trousers, and at over forty he still felt he had to keep pushing his dyed blond quiff back.

'Well, how are you?'

'I've been having nightmares again . . .'

The doctor was leafing through Max's medical notes.

'. . . red wine spilling on a white carpet. It's hell for me, can you understand that?'

'Hm. Well, we have here the contrast X-ray of your gastro-intestinal tract. Your duodenal bend, I'm afraid, is spreading and your stomach is displaced. The amylase concentration in your urine confirms that there's an acute drainage obstruction. Are you married? Any children?'

'No, I live on my own. My parents, sad to say, are already . . .'

'That makes it a lot easier. You should go straight into a pain-control clinic.'

'Why? I'm not in any pain.'

'You see, that's just what I'm trying to explain. The pain will come.'

'Why? What do you mean?'

'The fact is, and I'm afraid I cannot conceal it from you, you are suffering from carcinoma of the pancreas at an advanced stage.'

'I don't understand.'

The doctor was turning the information he provided into a kind of quiz. It seemed to make matters somehow easier for him.

'Pancreatic cancer, very difficult to diagnose, and when it's found it's usually too late. I'm afraid that's the case here.'

All the colour drained from Max's face.

'What are you talking about?' he managed to say.

'Those stomach pains, your weight loss. That was the cause. You already have metastases in the bones, in your case most of all in the spine.'

'Meaning what?'

'Meaning you'll suffer severe pain. But that won't be all. You may get swollen legs, thromboses, jaundice, alternate diarrhoea and constipation, nausea and vomiting.'

Dr Deckstein pushed the hair back from his forehead and reinforced his remarks by saying, 'It will be especially painful at the end.'

At this point the doctor had rehearsed a display of sympathy. He held his hand out to Max across his desk. Max ignored it.

'The fact is,' explained Dr Deckstein, withdrawing his hand

again, 'when the pain begins you won't be able to stand it without medical assistance and a good many drugs. That's why I do urge you to go into a clinic specializing in pain management.'

He looked around on his desk for a referral form, chattering on all the time about carcinoma of the pancreas. He seemed to have entirely forgotten that the pancreas sitting opposite him had something else attached to it, namely Max. Max now stood up without another word and walked out of the surgery.

The world had turned dark blue. The ten TV sets in the window of the electrical goods shop were flickering brightly, the presenter was waltzing with a studio guest, he turned and laughed. Max stared at him, clung to that picture. It made him feel dizzy. His displaced stomach heaved, the mush inside his head went round and round, he swayed. But his face was still set rigid even when he wept, a dry and motionless weeping. His tears crumbled on his jacket like dandruff. Little beads of sweat formed on his forehead, his lips trembled. He felt a strong urge to throw up. The TV presenter was still dancing and laughing. Max had to get out of here!

Walking stiffly, wild-eyed, he crossed the street, ignoring the traffic. Cars braked, hooted, drivers swore. Max saw and heard none of it.

Now he was standing at the wrought-iron gate of the beer garden, and pushed at it. It opened, he went in. With jerky movements, rigid as a robot, he began putting the chairs back in their proper places, six at every table, two each at the long sides, one each at the short sides. At right angles, with the same distance from the edge of the table to the back of each chair.

He worked first calmly, then faster and more frantically. Finally he ran back and forth among the tables, picked up chairs, rearranged them, always straight, always at right angles, as if it were his life he had to straighten out.

Tables tipped over; he hurt himself without feeling it. Max didn't see the people standing on the other side of the fence gaping. He didn't feel his tears, or the sweat running down his body.

At last the first sounds came out of his mouth. First he whimpered like a puppy, then he yapped out his grief. 'No no no no no. No experience, no life at all.'

Max was a loner. No woman had ever been close to him, no child had ever sat on his lap. He'd never summoned up the nerve for it. What if the woman left him one day? Taking the child? So he'd kept quiet, he'd done nothing, he had sat at his desk like a good boy – alone. And now he was finished. All washed up.

In wild despair and fury, Max picked up the last chair in both hands, raised it high above his head, and smashed it down as hard as he could on the edge of a table.

The wood broke to pieces, flying through the air.

As Max staggered towards the gate, a woman watching him shouted that he'd have to pay for the chair.

'With my life,' whispered Max.

Snot was running from his nose and over his lips. He raised his arm and wiped his face with his sleeve.

'With my life.'

*B*efore the Wall came down, Emma's farm had been at the back of beyond; now, after reunification, it was in the heart of Germany. The border between East and West was sorely missed by the people on both sides of it. Those electric fences and automatic firing devices had done such a nice, neat job of killing hares. Their bodies were found lying in the danger area known as the Death Strip on the eastern side in the morning, and the comrades regularly chucked them over to the western side, where the capitalist farmers said thank you for their Sunday lunch by throwing back bananas wrapped in silk stockings.

The district was known as Hessian Siberia, an accurate description. If you wanted to find any hospitality, kindness and tolerance here, you had to bore deep holes in the pack ice like a Russian angler out fishing.

Strangers who stayed for any length of time did so as accident victims in the local hospital. The magnificent avenues of trees along the highway guaranteed that the hospital beds were full. No one stopped off here of their own free will except Dutch tourists briefly using the coffee machine on their journey south.

The most tranquil souls hereabouts were to be found in the inns, where men would sit in silent companionship over their Pils, always in the same attitude.

The only fashions to reach this part of the country came not in the form of dresses or skirts, but in deciding which variety of spirits the locals would get tanked up on every season, always with beer as a chaser. There had been the apple brandy era, the peach spirits phase, the cola and rum season, and once, after the Countrywomen's Institute had come back from a study trip to Hanover, there was even a piña colada epoch. Wine was drunk only in the senior citizens' home, and if it was sweet and as sticky as jelly it was considered a fine vintage.

Good, filling food was eaten: meat and sausages, potatoes, air-dried ham, game with pear halves and cranberries. Salad stuff was all right for decoration, but it had to be swimming in sunflower oil and wine vinegar. Vegetables were cooked until they were as soggy as the *sauce hollandaise* in which they were drowned.

People were hospitable at wedding-eve parties, at weddings themselves, round-number birthdays and funerals. Any surprise visit in between was regarded as an ambush. Freshly baked sugar-cake was swiftly hidden away in the larder, pancakes still warm from the pan were concealed under teacloths, sausages and ham deposited in the bread bin. If your guests absolutely would not leave, you put a jar of salted breadsticks on the table and offered them raspberry syrup diluted with tap water.

You ate fish only if your false teeth were broken. Unless you'd been able to catch a few dozen trout in the neighbouring villages' fishponds. They were not baked or grilled, but smoked and eaten on fresh bread. Farmers built fish-smokers specially for these stolen trout. Home-caught fish never tasted so good.

Matriarchy was the rule in these parts. Men showed off in hunting parties, at rifle clubs, at the regulars' tables in the inns, in the fire brigade or at village meetings. But the women had the real say. Between them, they decided which of their husbands should be village mayor or chairman of the parish council. When the men should be sent to cut the wheat, and when to go to C & A in town.

The outward sign of female supremacy was the women's dress sizes, which began at size 16 and could easily go up to size 32. These large ladies were known as 'Whoppers'. The girth of a Whopper was indicated by spreading the arms out as far as they could go.

Such corpulence was acquired through the consumption of dreamily delicious home-made tarts and cakes: walnut cream or kiwi cream tarts, Frankfurt ring cake, chocolate and bilberry cake, cream puffs. They were lovingly baked over a period of several days for festive occasions, when they were decorated and served. For a company of guests who also had to put back an enormous amount of potatoes and meat, vegetables smothered in sauce and salad swimming in dressing in the same evening, you allowed half a tart or cake per person.

The women managed the money, paying out pocket-money to men. But Whoppers were such an incentive to work hard that a farmer whose wife had died before her time was sure to go bust unless he found a new wife to mistreat him within the year. If he didn't, he would have his mother back like a millstone around his neck again.

*M*ax had recovered his self-control only a little way from the beer garden. He blew his nose, mopped the sweat from his face, combed his hair, looked straight ahead and marched off. The emergency powers of his mind had come into force: his backbone had taken over at the helm from his brain. His body and emotions had switched to autopilot. Not a look to left or right, just on and on at a brisk pace for kilometres on end.

When he reached the garage hours later, he slunk into the office without letting anyone see him. He put his empty head down on his desk. His arms hung down, limp, and he stared at the wall, his eyes wide. If there had been a pistol lying beside him, you might have thought he was about to put a bullet through his head.

Max had known his boss and friend Hans since before they were born: their mothers had gone into labour simultaneously and brought their babies into the world at exactly the same time. Two Aries babies, Aries in the ascendant, the Sun in the first house, Mars in the fifth, the Moon in the ninth, Saturn and

Venus in the twelfth. Hans liked to say, and often did, that if you wanted to show what humbug astrology was then the two friends were living proof of it. Hans was ambitious, impulsive, loved danger and adventure, a real Aries. If asked to describe Max, he would say laconically, 'Oh well, Max. You mean *Max*? He's different.'

Their mothers had pushed their prams through the streets together, and later presided over the same sandbox, where Hans hit Max on the head with his spade and Max made no comment, didn't even yell.

Hans copied from Max in school for ten years. In the end he actually got better reports, because he could talk nineteen to the dozen. He didn't know much, but he presented his ignorance so cleverly that all the teachers, without exception, thought him a bright lad.

Max couldn't decide what he wanted to be, so Hans simply found jobs for them both. During their training as HGV drivers Max saw to the theory, Hans repaired the trucks. Then Hans used a legacy to open his own garage and gave Max a job in it. Hans was the car dealer, Max the accountant.

Hans went on copying from Max. When he wanted to show off and impress a woman, he liked to borrow Max's lifestyle. He rabbited on about his love of classical music, which in fact was all Max's, because good women are mad about Handel and Grieg. He made out that Max's recipes were his, because women go even wilder with admiration if a man cooks for them. What woman is ever admired for her cooking? Exactly! But guys who can cook, however fat, ugly and old they are, get to be TV stars.

Max loved music and cooking, but he didn't talk about it – he let Hans profit from his abilities. On a Monday he would listen to stories of the women they had captivated, and felt glad that nothing, as usual, had happened to him personally at the weekend.

The car showroom had opened hours ago.

'Tell you what, madam,' Hans was saying, beguiling his first customer of the day, 'this one's a lucky find for anyone wanting a good, sound used car.'

The lady had a spare tyre around her hips that would have kept her afloat in the English Channel, whereas the car Hans was trying to talk her into buying was tiny. Hans was an artist – every sales pitch became a real performance. The more difficult it was, the more he enjoyed it. Would he manage to get the fat lady into the little car? What tactics should he employ? How about this . . . ?

'The previous owner is a senior master at the Holy Ghost Grammar School.'

He observed the customer's eyes and gestures for any reaction.

'He didn't really want to get rid of the car, but he's gone to Togo for three years. He's . . .' Hans searched for the best verb. Not gone there, not flown there, not been sent there. He needed something more to account for Togo, suggesting higher status. Been dispatched? No, sounded too much like the Foreign Office.

'. . . been appointed to Africa.'

The customer looked at Hans with wonder and amazement.

She didn't say anything, but her eyes were pleading with him to tell her more. Every customer wanted to be told a story, every last one of them! And Hans had an unlimited supply of stories in stock. Writers and used car salesmen – they both have that talent, but writers stay poor. Hans, on the other hand, got rich.

'To a mission station there.'

'Ooh, really?' she piped up. 'They need a senior teacher at the mission station?'

'They certainly do, madam. And his car stays here.'

'That's ever so interesting.'

There was a price tag stuck on the windscreen of the car. It was an outrageous demand for ten thousand euros. The woman stared at this figure. Too much.

'As you saw from the forecourt, the car costs seven thousand.'

The woman's forefinger pointed at the price tag. 'It says ten there.'

Hans looked, and actually turned pale. Actors spend ages rehearsing how to shed spontaneous tears; Hans could even go pale on demand!

'Oh dear,' he said, dismayed. 'My mistake. I was thinking of the other car, the one back there.'

He clapped his hand to his mouth in horror.

'I'm so sorry, yes, of course, this car is priced at ten thousand euros.'

His voice assumed a deferential note. He was trying to persuade himself to feel afraid of her. Inside, Hans begged, Please don't punish me!

Meanwhile, unnoticed, he pressed an alert button. A light

was switched on in Dagmar's office. Her signal to come on stage and play her part in the game.

Hans was playing things down. 'I mean, the car's really a little too small for you, and then I've had other offers . . .'

Dagmar tottered into the showroom on high heels and in a black suit, playing the part of the dominating boss. If they made a sale her performance, complete with horn-rimmed glasses, got her a ten per cent commission, and she earned more that way than she did with her secretarial work in the outer office. Her Austrian accent, however, was not a fake but came from Vienna, where Dagmar had grown up.

Hans clasped his hands and begged, 'Oh, please, madam! Here comes my boss.'

'Then she can decide.'

'Oh no, please!'

Dagmar did not retreat when the customer marched up to the supposed boss. 'First I'm told that car costs seven thousand, now your salesman suddenly wants ten thousand.'

Dagmar glanced at the price tag. 'Says ten there, like you can see.'

'That's not what he quoted me! A quote is a quote!' The woman's voice rose.

Dagmar turned to Hans and said sternly, 'What offer did you make the lady?'

'I'm ever so sorry, ma'am,' said Hans pathetically. 'I made a mistake! It was an accident.'

'You said *how much*?'

'Seven thousand. By mistake!'

Dagmar turned back to the woman and said, never turning

a hair, 'Well, you got a bargain there and no mistake. Like you said, a quote's a quote. Yup, the car's yours for seven thousand.'

And so saying she turned an angry glance on Hans, a glance designed to make the customer guess he'd pay dearly for it later. The woman grinned saucily. She'd snapped up a bargain, and in the process she had quite forgotten whether she really wanted the car or not. The little car wasn't worth the money. Its gearbox had been wrecked, not by a senior teacher but by a novice woman driver.

As the customer was driving proudly away from the forecourt with her new acquisition, and Hans and Dagmar were celebrating their success – 'Ooh, Hans, what a one you are! The things you do think up!' – a man in a dark suit got out of a Jaguar. He entered the showroom, greeted Hans with a brotherly kiss, put an arm around his shoulders and led the boss into his own office, not without taking a good look at Dagmar's behind. Dagmar wasn't sure whether her boss was letting this man take the dominant role for some ulterior motive, or whether Hans was in fact secretly afraid of the guy.

The stranger entered the office. Since Max was still slumped there, looking as if he'd been shot, the guest, who had plenty of experience in criminal matters, crossed himself in the Orthodox Christian manner, at the same time calling upon the Devil for help. *'Boshe moi, tchorti shto.'*

Hans put an arm around Max's shoulders and shook him.

'Max? Are you OK?'

'No.'

Max got to his feet, turned to stone but still ready to function.

In the office, the man put a plastic bag full of dollar bills down on Hans's desk. Max was to count them while Hans conducted negotiations. The man was speaking in English, badly and rolling his Rs. This time, he said, he wanted a red Ferrari. Hans promised him one. No problem!

'Fifty thousand,' Max announced the result. He wanted nothing to do with this deal. It was Hans's business, Max just counted the money.

When the guy had finally left, Max stowed the dollar bills away in the safest hiding place there was in this office. Not in the box with the petty cash, not in the conspicuously large safe. Max rolled up the plastic bag, opened the door of a small washroom, bent down to the cat-litter tray there, rooted around with disgust in the litter, which was full of cat shit, and buried the box so deeply that it was out of sight.

He heard Hans in the office asking what was up with him, where he had been for so long, while at the same time he picked up the phone and tapped in a number.

'I went to see the doctor,' Max called back.

'And?' asked Hans.

Max, still crouching in front of the litter tray, said loud and clear, his voice very serious, 'And I'm going to die. Soon.'

He stood up, looked at his only friend and tried to catch his eye. He even went right up to him. Hans didn't seem to have made his connection. He put the receiver down and clapped Max absent-mindedly on the shoulder.

'Well, that's fine, then!'

*E*mma's house was hundreds of years old, a half-timbered building with black beams and whitewashed walls crumbling in many places. Virginia creeper clambered over it, weighing heavily down on the walls. It looked like a place under a magic spell. The farm lay among gently rolling hills, meadows and forests where mushrooms grew profusely, the oldest oaks stood, and the brothers Grimm had collected their best stories.

An old chestnut tree stood in the farmyard, giving shade in hot summer weather. Emma fed the chestnuts to the red deer in winter, for it could turn cold and icy here.

A long, low pigsty lay on one side of the farmyard, a tall barn on the other, and beyond it was the dung heap. This was the hereditary residence of the rooster, who would strike a fine attitude on top of it, craning his tough body and crowing cock-a-doodle-do over the farm and the fields. He woke Emma punctually early in the morning, and picked himself a hen every full hour on the dot. No one needed a watch around here.

The farm buildings were left open during the day. Chickens

pecked about between the tractor and the harrow, and scratched for worms on the banks of the stream. The pigs strolled in a huge meadow. They had made themselves a muddy place to wallow in close to the stream, behind the house and right under a mighty beech tree.

Emma's bathhouse stood beside the stream about fifty metres further on. A German from Russia had once built it for her in exchange for meat and sausages. Emma was thus the only person in the district to have a Russian *banja*, a kind of sauna, and she treasured it. She heated both the bathhouse and the farmhouse with timber that she herself cut down, sawed and chopped up in the forest.

Every living thing here lived by every other; the chickens did well on Emma's vegetable scraps, the vegetables did well on the chicken dung, the rooster did well out of the hens. And possibly vice versa too. No one could really know, and the hens expressed no opinion.

Emma made her living from the pigs and the wonderful sausages she made from them, and the pigs in turn ate Emma's rubbish. Emma was bound up in this cycle, she was a part of the whole and entirely at home in it. But imprisoned in it too, because she understood nothing about other cycles in the world outside the farm.

Emma herself couldn't remember just how she came to begin using the moped that way. It was her father's old Zündapp, and she had inherited it when he died. Her father used to ride it along the winding road through the forest to the town. But

Emma didn't need to go that way. She knew no one outside her village, and didn't dare go to town. She would dare just about anything else, but not that.

However, Emma rode the moped. She had laid out her own track for it beside the house. Tarred by herself. It appeared to be a pointless stretch of road, beginning in the green grass, running for a thousand metres, and then coming to an end just before it reached the tall fir trees. Of course she had no permit to build roads herself, but what did that matter? Henner was the law around here. No other police officer wanted to be posted to these godforsaken parts. If Henner told the authorities in town that the countryside here was at peace, then all was well.

So Emma pushed her old Zündapp laboriously up the path through the fields to the beginning of her private road. She turned the moped to face the way she'd be riding, sat on it, started the engine and let it warm up.

Emma's farm was several hundred metres from the village itself. But Henner could hear that *brrm brrm* coming through the open window into his poky office. He thoughtfully shook his head and smiled. He liked what Emma was doing. He liked everything about her.

When Emma revved up her little two-stroke engine, it was a kind of signal to the villagers. They knew what it meant. The sound struck up several times a week. Everyone could hear it. Most people ignored it, but it got some of them very agitated. Henner's old mother, for instance, cursed 'that slut' and lit two cigarettes at once in her rage. The baker listened to the sound with avid attention, but his wife made the children come indoors. As for the potato farmer, the sound stimulated him tremendously. He took a break from work, leaned against his potato sacks in the middle of the field, and gave himself up to pleasure.

Henner took a break too, but unlike the potato farmer's it was a sandwich break. Only a good liver-sausage sandwich could really relax him, and the hottest thing Henner dreamed of was the mustard on the liver sausage.

Emma stepped on the gas, the moped raced away full tilt. Her old Zündapp had a wonderfully unbalanced flywheel, which set the leather saddle vibrating strongly after just three hundred metres. Emma kept her back straight, held the handlebars well away from her with her arms outstretched, and pushed her nether regions far enough forward to feel those sweet little tremors of strong arousal. After only six hundred metres Emma had a violent orgasm. She closed her eyes as she came and rode almost blind for three hundred metres. Her arms held the handlebars out ahead to keep on the track, but her soul did the opposite. She had to force herself to open her eyes when the trees at the end of her road came racing towards her at dangerous speed. On the last few metres of asphalt the tyres were sliding, the moped began to shake, and it skidded off the tarmac into the mud. As usual, Emma managed to stop the Zündapp only at the very last minute. Suddenly all was still, except for a blackbird singing in the fir trees.

As soon as the sounds of the fast-revving engine had died away, the villagers calmed down. Henner felt satisfied; the baker took a deep breath, inhaling the smell of his warm loaves; the potato farmer had fertilized his field. Only Henner's mother and the baker's wife were spitting nicotine and brimstone.

Emma turned her lovely moped and rode back in gentle curves, feeling all relaxed. She heard beautiful sounds just after she came. Her mind was wrapped in cotton wool. Strong arms held her close but didn't control her. Everything will be all right, she thought, the sky will rain soft feathers.

*W*ell, *that's fine, then* . . . Hans hadn't even been listening to him. No one was listening! The tears started flowing again. Pouring out of his face. He wasn't used to that, he didn't want it. Not here in the office! How was he to take his mind off all this? He got up, walked around the showroom, stroking the cars on display. The beautiful paint soothed him. Max blew his nose and breathed in deeply. He could still do that. His body was obeying him. For now.

He was alive. How would he spend his last few weeks?

Not in this garage, anyway.

He went through the showroom and out, walked down the street. Thinking, searching his meagre life for something good, something to make it worth going on living. When had his life been good?

It was good while his parents were still alive.

And he'd once won a prize in a competition, years ago. That was good too. A trip to the Caribbean, the Gulf of Mexico. First prize, and to start with he hadn't even wanted to go!

What if he were to drown in the sea?

'How come you can't swim?' Hans asked.

'Because I'm afraid of water.'

'Just jump in and try it!'

'I'm not going into the water until I can swim!'

'Oh, really, that's absurd! In the water is the only place to learn to swim.'

'That's my problem, not yours!'

Hans put his head in his hands. Max went on moaning.

'What if the plane crashes? What if I catch malaria or typhoid? What if I don't like it there?'

Hans shouted at him. 'What if, what if, what if . . . you're getting me down! Have you lost your marbles? Why did you go in for the competition in the first place? Now you've won you're flying out there, or I'm going to kick your arse!'

He even threatened to break off their friendship and fire Max if he didn't accept the prize.

Those were the best two weeks of Max's life. He stayed on the island of Holbox, north of Quintana Roo, in a lovely round Mayan hut thatched with palm leaves. Bamboo furniture, a tropical wood floor. A ventilator in the ceiling, a mosquito net over the bed, a blue-and-white hammock on the airy veranda. What he enjoyed most was lying in the hammock looking out at the wonderful Caribbean sea. Such beautiful blue light, such marvellous colours, the turquoise water! And the pelicans! Oh, the pelicans!

Max spent hours on the beach watching the pelicans. They were dark-coloured here, an almost ugly grey-black. They'd have looked like vultures if it hadn't been for the typical pelican pouches under their big beaks. They flew over the water looking for fish to eat. And as soon as they spotted a fish swimming unsuspectingly around, they dived straight down to the sea. They folded their wings and went into the water head first. It slapped and splashed as they hit it. They didn't catch much, perhaps one fish in every ten dives, when they either swallowed the fish at once or stored it in their pouches. And then they were off again, up in the air, scouting around, dive-bombing the water. The waves splashed.

Max never tired of watching them. He'd have liked to fall straight into life at long last like the pelicans, making a big splash. He had discovered something there in Mexico. But once he was back in Germany, his *what-if-itis* rambled all over his Caribbean dreams, choking them to death.

Now Max walked through the town, kilometre after kilometre, until he found himself outside the travel agency. He plucked up his courage and went in.

'To Mexico. For some weeks, yes. Several weeks, I hope. I think three months should do it. Expensive. Yes, of course. I realize that. I'll bring you the money tomorrow. American dollars, will that be all right? Thank you. See you tomorrow, then.'

Next day, which was Saturday, Max waited for dark. He had a pair of jeans with the price tag still attached. He'd been keeping them for some day later. Some day later was now, so he tore the price tag off and put on the jeans, then a T-shirt with a leather jacket over it that he had also bought some time or other and never worn.

He packed a few things in his little travelling bag. Put his passport in his pocket. In fact it was valid for only a few more months, but that ought to be enough, he thought bitterly.

In the living room, he took the photo of his parents out of its wooden frame and put it in his wallet. Then he looked round his immaculately furnished apartment one last time. His father had designed it so beautifully and harmoniously that he himself could never think of anything new, and so it had remained unchanged for decades.

He was just about to close the front door behind him when he thought better of it. He went back into the living room, over to his dining table, and tipped over one of his elegantly curved Thonet chairs. Left it lying helplessly on the floor, smiled at this small victory, and left his apartment for ever.

Max had parked his car behind the workshop. He looked around to see whether by any chance there was still someone here. But it was all the same as usual. The showroom with the cars was brightly illuminated, while all was dark in the office.

He crossed the forecourt towards the building, as he had done thousands of times before, but this time his heart was in his mouth. He unlocked the door and went into the garage with a torch, like a burglar.

He took a step inside the office. The beam of the flashlight searched for the desk, found the telephone, found the safe which was only a dummy. Then, suddenly, he felt something touching his ankles. Max screamed and retreated.

'Miaooow.'

'Damn cat!'

His circulation lost its rhythm, something inside his ribcage hurt. To calm himself, he sat down in Hans's leather armchair, put his hand on his heart, and breathed deliberately slowly.

At the same time, Hans was meeting a thin young broker aged only twenty-five in a deserted car park on the motorway. The young Ferrari owner was short of cash after speculating wildly and losing money. He had to think of something fast.

Hans bought the Ferrari from him. He'd have the serial number sanded off in the workshop, get the car resprayed, and his contact, a Belarusian, would take the car to Minsk. The fact that road conditions there would ruin it didn't bother the nouveau riche buyer, who had already wrecked other items in this price range. In the middle of the following week the little broker would report his car stolen and his insurance would pay up.

Max had jammed the torch under his arm, opened the washroom door, and rummaged around in the litter tray with distaste. The torch beam flickered erratically around the room, along the corridor wall and past the windows. Which is what Hans saw when he drove into the forecourt.

He immediately switched off the engine of the Ferrari so that no one could hear him. Raced straight into his office with berserk fury to catch the intruder in the act. In his haste he left the key in the ignition, and he avoided slamming the driver's door of the car so as not to make any noise.

Max heard him. He recognised Hans's footsteps. Rigid with terror, he clutched the plastic bag of money.

If only he'd done so-and-so! If only he'd not done such-and-such! Before he could even think what he was going to say or do now, he knew it was too late to make a break for it. Shaking, he hid behind the floor-length curtains, the dollar bills clutched firmly to his chest.

The intrepid Hans pushed his office door open and called at random, into the dark, 'Hands up! Police!'

Nothing moved. He switched the light on and looked round the room. The cat padded straight over to Max's feet, which were peeping out from behind the curtain.

Hans drew the curtain back, and the two men stared at each other. Then meek, nice, quiet Max, Max who would always do anything for Hans, who wanted and asked for nothing, Max, of all people, took aim without warning. Flailed out with the bag and hit his friend's left cheek so hard that Hans was taken by surprise and fell over. Max made good use of that brief moment. He raced out, and had enough presence of mind to lock the door behind him in the nick of time.

Hans got to his feet and thundered on the door with his fist.

'Open up, what's the matter with you, are you off your head or what?'

But Max was crossing the forecourt, saw the Ferrari with its door open and leaped in behind the wheel. He threw the bag of money down on the passenger seat beside him and roared away.

The force of so much horsepower pressed his back firmly into the leather upholstery as he went from zero to a hundred within a few seconds. He wasn't used to it. He convulsively clutched the wheel and tried to come to terms with this crazy car and get the speed down to seventy kilometres per hour, at least in town. It was really difficult, driving slowly in this Ferrari. What an amazing beast!

Hans managed to get free. He climbed through the window. He was so furious to find the Ferrari gone that he kicked a rubbish bin. It fell out of its holder and clattered to the ground of the forecourt.

He made for Max's car, which still had the key in it too. Now he just had to try catching up with the Ferrari, Max and his money in this old banger. What the hell had got into the guy?

Just as Max was driving out of town the heavens opened. The rain was like a monsoon. It was pouring down in buckets, water pelted against the windscreen. The windscreen wipers were severely overworked. Max was forced to slow down. But Hans was ready to take risks, and he was the better driver. He caught up with Max as he reached the outskirts of the forest. The road grew narrower here, winding up into the mountains. Driving became difficult for Max. Hans was close behind, overtook him! Came to a halt at an angle halfway across the road, trying to stop him. But Max edged past and stepped on the gas. He knew he had to go faster. But he could see hardly anything except the rain. Hans turned, caught up again, even nudged the Ferrari's back bumper from behind. Then, at last, Max shot off as fast as he could go. He just made it round several bends by the skin of his teeth.

Then came a place where the Ferrari simply wouldn't take the bend any more. Max was steering correctly, but the tyres refused to obey. With Max inside it, the car shot through the trees and down a slope.

But Hans drove past, deeper into the forest. Many kilometres further on he gave up the chase. The ground seemed to have opened to swallow up Max and the Ferrari. Hans turned the car around and drove back, looking for clues as best he could in the darkness, but he found nothing. The place where Max and the Ferrari had cut a narrow swathe through the forest couldn't be seen by night. Cursing, Hans drove back to town for now.

Max breathed a sigh of relief. It was over at last. Turning criminal, making his getaway to Mexico, dying in turquoise-coloured water? It was not to be. He was dying here in the forest. The trees moved past him as if in slow motion. A fascinating flight. Very slowly, the car swung round. Max took it all in very clearly. As the Ferrari crashed down the slope, turning several somersaults, he sat strapped inside it, noting calmly that at least this was an exciting way to go.

He waited for not just the trees but his whole life to pass before his eyes within seconds, but that particular film didn't seem to be on the programme. All he saw was a pressure-cooker. Boiling on a stove. That was all.

Unspectacular, a death like this. If he'd only known dying was so easy, he wouldn't have wasted his whole life fearing it.

Pressure-cooker?

The metal of the Ferrari cracked apart, the windows fell out, bursting like soap bubbles, tiny splinters of glass shone with colour. A few small trees had been hit too. But not Max. Only at the end did he receive a heavy blow on his temple as a stout branch struck him. The wreck of the car had reached the bottom of the slope and now lay still on the land near an isolated farmhouse. The broken radiator hissed, the hot engine steamed in the rain.

*E*mma was brusquely woken by the sound of the car's
impact. She went to the window and saw headlights
shining at the bottom of the slope in the heavy rain. On the
spur of the moment, she put on her grandfather's enormous
olive-green raincoat. Since it was longer than she was tall, she
dragged it along the floor behind her like a train. The raincoat
had a hood. She pulled the hood over her head and went out.

Emma looked at the wrecked car with no sense of panic,
without any alarm, simply curious and interested.

What a lovely car it had been! She walked around the red
heap of metal at her leisure, marvelling at the strange engine
sticking out of the battered bonnet, so very different from the
engine of her tractor.

Only now did she notice the unconscious man behind the
steering wheel. Emma touched him gently, put a hand to his
ribcage. The man didn't move. He wasn't bleeding either.
Emma felt his carotid artery. He was alive.

'A man!'

Heaven had finally delivered one, and of course he had to
be damaged already. Broken in transit. But better a damaged

43

man than no man at all, thought Emma. He'll soon get better!

She undid the safety belt, took the stranger under the armpits and hauled him out of the car. The hood slipped off her head, and her hair was drenched by the streaming rain. So was the man's body. Summoning up all her strength, she picked him up, slung him over her shoulder like half of a pig's carcase, and carried him through the doorway of her house.

In the kitchen, she put him down on the table. There was still a plate on it, and the plate fell to the floor and broke. The noise didn't wake the man, but all the same he was breathing. Emma removed her raincoat and filled an enamel bowl with water. She stripped off his wet clothes and dropped them under the table. Then she rubbed him dry without shame or embarrassment. He had bruised himself all over in the accident, but nothing seemed to be seriously wrong.

Emma ran up to her bedroom, threw her quilt off the bed and ran downstairs again. She slung the naked body over her shoulder once more and carried the man upstairs, where she tipped him off her shoulder, laid him carefully on the bed and covered him up. She felt his pulse, listened to his breathing. Everything seemed to be in order. It was just that he was still unconscious. So she left him alone for the time being.

Downstairs she put the raincoat on again and went back to the wreck of the car to look for his things. He had no travelling bag, no suitcase, no briefcase. Just a plastic bag on the passenger seat. Unhesitatingly, she looked inside it.

'Dear God, please make me rich or happy,' she had prayed

44

at her open window every evening for years and years. Always sending her prayers straight up to the sky, although recently only out of habit. And now this! She took the bag into the slaughterhouse, where it was dry and bright. Opened it and looked inside again. Lots of foreign banknotes. Dollar bills! It said THE UNITED STATES OF AMERICA on them. With faces of men she had never seen, but Emma knew what dollar bills looked like from TV. Wads of banknotes as thick as books. What a wonderful feeling!

Was she going to fetch Henner now and ask for his help?

No. Not she.

Rich *or* happy? Within a mere half an hour of her life, she had a bag full of money in her hand and a naked man in her bed. Rich *and* happy. She could hardly believe it! She needed money and she wanted a man. Now she had them both, and she was going to keep them safe.

She took the plastic bag and hid it in the boar's sty behind his trough. He was dangerous – only Emma would venture in here. Now she just had to make sure no one could know about her theft.

She fetched a can of mixed oil and petrol from the tool shed, poured it over the stranger's car and then set it alight. The flames shot high into the air.

All the villagers were asleep except for Henner's mother, who was suffering from insomnia as usual. So she heard the strange crackling and hissing, went to the window, and saw a red glow in the night sky above Emma's farm.

A spiteful smile distorted her face. Had Emma's wiring given up the ghost? Or maybe a member of the fire brigade had been trying his hand at arson again? In these parts volunteer firemen usually started the fires themselves.

Henner's mother saw the leaping flames, and had no intention of raising the alarm. It would have disturbed her Henner's sleep. Full of curiosity, the old woman watched the flickering light. She regarded Emma as a slut, if only for what she did with that moped. She had to protect her Henner from a woman like that – it was a good mother's duty. Because Henner had suffered from asthma ever since he was a little boy. The doctor had warned her that a happy marriage could be the death of Henner. So now there was a fire at Emma's farm. The old woman lit herself a cigarette. Henner belonged to her. She had borne him in pain and brought him up herself. She still washed his shirts and darned his socks today. She was the best woman in the world for her son, so why would he need another one? Exactly. So there. Let it burn, good night and good riddance!

Emma had rubbed her hair dry in her kitchen. She took a T-shirt off the washing line. To be on the safe side she threw on a brightly coloured overall too, just in case he opened his eyes after all.

Up in her bedroom she pulled a chair up beside the bed, sat down and examined the stranger. She nudged him again, but he didn't move. He was still unconscious. Once again she checked his pulse, his breathing. The man was fast asleep. There'd never been a strange man in her bed before. Henner, yes, but she'd known him forever.

Emma laid a finger cautiously on his face and ran it along his high hairline. She looked at his hair. It was still all brown. Looked at his scalp. There was no dirt or dandruff on it.

She traced every single line on his brow with her forefinger. He had a lot of lines there, six or seven of them. Deep lines, too. He was not a cheerful man, he had troubles. The skin just under his eyes was swollen, slightly rimmed with blue. Like a doctor, Emma pulled his lower eyelid down, saw little red veins on the yellow eyeball. His liver was in a bad way. Did he drink too much?

Then she raised his upper lip and inspected his teeth, as if he were a horse she was planning to buy. She approved of those teeth. She smelled him. No bad breath.

She looked in his ears, dug the little finger of her left hand into them, but no wax came out under her nail. She looked up his nose, stood up and leaned right down so that she could see into his nostrils properly. A few small hairs in them, but no snot. Satisfied, she leaned back and examined his face from a distance.

She took his right hand in both hers. Stroked the inside of it, turned the hand over, felt the back of his hand. No calluses, no broken skin. The stranger's hands were soft and delicate. Hers, on the other hand, when she looked at them for purposes of comparison, were broad, strong and cracked. She had great, rough paws beside his. A city man, then.

She pushed the quilt aside and stroked him from the curve of his shoulder over his sparse chest hair and down to his upper belly. She couldn't feel much muscle, but not a lot of spare flab either. More of a medium-sized yielding layer of fat surrounding him, making him a little rounded. Emma came so close to him that his chest hair tickled her face. And at that moment she was magically attracted by his smell, let her nose go exploring and found the best place in a little indentation close to his shoulder blade at the base of his throat. Here he smelled so delicious that Emma burrowed her nose into the small hollow, sniffed, drew the aroma in deeply, couldn't get enough of it. She knew him by his smell. This was her man.

Emma wrapped him in the quilt again, leaned back and allowed her thoughts to wander. Then she suddenly raised the far end of the quilt and inspected his feet. She separated his toes and sniffed between them. Felt the nail bed, stroked his heels. Everything was smooth, perfectly clean and well tended.

Emma always went barefoot out of doors in summer. She raised her right foot and put it beside his to compare them. Her foot was dirty and horny. His was white, and as soft as his hands.

Emma took her foot off the bed and made herself comfortable again. Her eyes moved over the quilt and stopped in the middle of his body.

She stared at the billowing quilt, grinning with the same sense of daring as the six-year-old girl had once felt in the maize field. Slowly she raised the quilt until she had a good view of him. As discreetly as possible for a woman who was also a farmer, she peered at it from a distance.

His penis was unconscious too, lying on top of his thigh to the left. Emma seemed to like it, for a tender, contented smile stole over her face. Carefully, she lowered the quilt again and rose from her chair. Shook up the feathers in the quilt again,

48

affectionately stroked his forehead, kissed him softly on his lips, put the light out and left her own bedroom, swinging her hips slightly.

Emma had a favourite place in the straw, and she slept there tonight. Its three walls had been built with bales of straw around a window in the barn, and the floor was carpeted with fresh hay.

Even as a child she used to lie up here. It made her grandfather furious, but then everything made him furious. When he suspected she was there in the straw he would bellow with rage and threaten her with the sharp-pronged pitchfork. He claimed that she wrecked the bales of straw by playing about. Even in old age he would climb the narrow steps to the loft, but Emma always managed to get away in time. She jumped out of the window and dropped three metres, to land on the muck heap just below it.

Up above the tyrant ranted, while Emma sat down there in the dirt, laughing and making faces at the old man. That gave him the daily dose of adrenalin he needed to boost his circulation.

'You imp of Satan, you! I'll beat the living daylights out of you. We'll see who's master in this house when I get my hands on you.'

Tonight Emma had left the barn window open, because she loved to look at the starry sky before she fell asleep.

But it was a cool night, and the bad dreams that regularly plagued Emma came tonight as usual. She restlessly tossed and turned and threw her quilt off. That woke her. She was freezing. She had forgotten the dream as soon as she opened her eyes, and only a miserable feeling remained. A sense of being guilty of something. She pulled the quilt back over her and heaped fragrant hay on top of it until she felt warmer. So she lay there, and her thoughts took wing over the dark horizon.

Every star in the sky a dollar bill. Dollars! Where was she going to exchange this foreign money?

What was she going to do with the man?

She must go to a bank in town. But she'd never been there! Here in the village they only had the post office savings bank, and the baker's wife, of all people, ran that.

How did the man get his ears so clean?

If she paid off her debts on the farm all of a sudden, Henner would wonder where the money came from. He wasn't just her friend, he was also a policeman.

How often did he trim the hairs in his nostrils?

The lottery! She'd say she won it on the lottery. But she'd never played the lottery. She didn't even know how.

Emma stroked her breasts and imagined his hands doing it. How exciting, a strange man in her bed! But suppose he was gone tomorrow? He had to stay.

A present? But Emma had no one to give her presents.

Suppose Henner found out?

Was the stranger different from Henner? Emma felt curious, so curious! She was already getting ideas about what she could do with her new, unknown man.

But suppose he left first? He mustn't leave, whatever happened!

Found it! She'd found the money!

But then the man could say it belonged to him. He'd be off, and her reward for finding it wouldn't be enough to save the farm.

Where had the man got all that money from anyway? And why put it in a plastic bag? Had he been playing the lottery himself? Got it as a present? Found it?

No, he'd stolen it. She wasn't a thief, *he* was – or at least he had been a thief first.

A thief, then. Well, fancy that! Criminals are supposed to be very good at making love. According to the TV.

She'd done well to burn that car. It meant the bag of money had been burnt too. So he'd think. So he must believe!

She wanted him to be a thief. Then she could keep the money. And he'd have to stay with her, she'd hide him and keep him here. She'd have her money and her man.

She'd heat the sauna for him tomorrow, he'd like that. She'd do all she could to make sure he liked it with her.

Her eyes were closing. The man and the money. Perfect.

It was all hers now. It belonged to her and no one else. Emma fell peacefully asleep in the wonderful hay and fragrant straw. Her grandfather was dead, luckily. Luckily they were all dead.

*W*hen Max woke up he was lying in a strange bed. A thick, feather-filled quilt was pressing him deep down into the soft mattress. The bedlinen, which had an old-fashioned lilac flower pattern, was old and faded. Max seemed to have been deeply unconscious, for he hadn't heard the rooster wake Emma hours ago.

He lay under the heavy quilt without moving and stared up. Above him, houseflies were playing Catch. Flying around at sharp angles. Setting off in another direction, flying back and then forward again, never stopping. He watched this game for a long time. He'd never seen anything like it.

Max moved nothing but his eyes. Looked to the right, where he saw an old doctor's bag without a clasp beside the bed. It was open and had newspapers, brochures and letters stacked inside it. The pile of papers was weighted down with a lamp that had no shade. He saw cups on the floor filled with mould in various stages of maturity from white to green, along with other rubbish. Also an open jar of face cream, perfume samples from the pharmacy, deformed root vegetables and a dried fly agaric fungus.

Opposite the bed he saw the last remains of a cupboard with items of clothing spilling out of it, all in stridently glaring colours. And to his left a bottle of beer lay on its side in its own puddle. Not red wine. But the carpet underneath it wasn't as beautiful as his, it was threadbare and greyish brown. Whether that was its original shade or the dirt of a hundred years he couldn't be sure from the bed. But the beer left no stains on it.

Max closed his eyes again, deeply grieved. He was in Hell, then. Died and gone straight to Hell, just like that.

However, when he moved he felt something. Bruises. His head. The back of his neck was horribly painful. Painful?

He was still alive! Max raised the quilt and saw that he was naked. Covered with blue and green marks. Someone must have taken all his clothes off. Dragged him here. Got him out of the car. He'd had an accident. He'd stolen money from Hans, he'd nicked a car, he wanted to go to Mexico and he was incurably ill. Was going to die a miserable death. Whoever had put him in this bed was no rescuer but an idiot.

If only he were dead!

Max tried to get up. His ribs! They hurt like hell. However, he got to his feet and supported himself on the edge of the bed. Looked for something to put on, drew a torn and yellowed net curtain aside, and peered out of the window. Was that blackish-brown lump down there by any chance the Ferrari?

Emma was in the bathhouse when she heard the man slamming the front door of the house. Here goes, she thought.

She stationed herself behind the sauna door and watched him through the little glass window.

He was wearing one of her overalls, the yellow one with the red flowers. She had to put her hand over her mouth to keep from laughing out loud. Hairy legs showed under the skirts of the overall. He looked like Rumpelstiltskin, and he was hopping about like Rumpelstiltskin too.

He was barefoot and didn't seem used to it. He obviously hated the dust, was hopping about in zigzags as if his feet wouldn't get so dirty that way. But that just made it worse. He trod in puddles, slipped on chicken shit, shouted and cursed. It was so funny. Emma's eyes feasted on the sight of him.

Finally he found what was left of the red car. Now he was hopping about even more crazily, higher and higher in the air. Voice rising to a squawk, he cried, 'Is that . . . is that . . . oh no! Why do I always . . . why, where?'

Emma was bent double with delight. Tears of laughter were running down her cheeks. That man, in her overall!

He was searching the car, he was looking for the money! When he realised that it was all burned he let out such a scream that it quite spoiled Emma's fun. She buttoned up her own overall decently, slipped into a pair of huge green wellies and went over the farmyard towards him.

Did that overall look as ridiculous on her too? For the first time she was seeing the garment on someone else, like a sausage skin splashed with colour and leaving the wearer's head, arms and legs sticking out. She had never felt ashamed of her clothes before. Now she did.

She stopped in front of him. He had lovely brown eyes.

'What happened?' he asked. 'What on earth happened?'

So saying, he waved his thin, gangling arms frantically in the air and howled uninhibitedly.

She felt like taking him in her arms and giving him the money back. But she needed it so badly. So she bowed to necessity and lied. Said that the car caught fire just after she'd dragged him out of it.

'How come the car caught fire? Why would it do that?'

Emma shrugged her shoulders. She didn't know why either, she said.

'Wasn't there something in the car? On the passenger seat?' asked the man.

'What kind of thing?' Emma scraped the toes of her boots in the dirt.

'Just something.'

He didn't say money. He didn't say a plastic bag. So he *had* stolen it, he was a thief. Good. That meant he wouldn't go away, he would have to hide. On her farm. She just had to go about it cleverly. Then he'd stay.

'It was raining buckets when I got you out. And as I was taking you into the house it suddenly caught fire all of its own accord.'

His eyes flashed. 'The car caught fire and it was raining at the same time?'

Emma shrugged again.

The man slumped down on the wooden block where chickens were beheaded. Sat in the dried chicken blood. What a good thing he didn't know . . . it would shock him so much he'd start crying again. Gradually Emma was recovering her confidence. It passed through her mind that he might say thank you. After all, she'd rescued him last night.

'Does it hurt anywhere?' she asked.

He shook his head.

'Do you want me to take you to a doctor or call one out?'

Once again he merely shook his head.

'Would you like to relax? I have a sauna – I've been heating it up. And there are some men's clothes in it for you. Would you like to put them on?'

He nodded, but didn't move.

'Come on, I'll show you.'

Emma had done her best. Had fried eggs and bacon. Put fresh milk on the kitchen table, with fragrant bread and coffee. The raspberry jam was made with fruit from her garden.

The man came into the kitchen in some of her late father's clothes, sat down at the table stiff as a poker, but didn't touch a thing.

'Help yourself, go on!'

He shook his head.

Emma looked at Max in the olive-green work clothes and saw an image of her father before her eyes. He'd worn a peaked cap in the same colour. The travelling pedlar Flachsmeier had brought this male counterpart to her overall. All the farmers hereabouts wore his cheap green cotton garments like a uniform.

'How was the sauna? Hot enough?'

He just shook his head again.

When no one could see him, neither his wife nor Emma's grandfather, her father had been almost affectionate. At such times he ran his hand through her hair. Not very often, but it happened. Those had been her happiest moments. Now a man was sitting there at the kitchen table in her father's clothes, a man whose naked body she already knew.

'You did use the sauna, didn't you?'

He said nothing.

'You didn't? What a shame. Your injuries aren't too bad for that. In fact it would do your bruises good.'

He sat there as if turned to stone. Staring ahead of him. Then he glanced in the direction of the stove, then in the direction of the larder, at the table, at the floor.

He muttered something about Mao. Emma had no idea what he meant by that. It made no sense. She felt nervous. What was the matter with him?

Max was perched on the edge of the chair, his hands in his lap, his legs pressed together, his shoulders hunched as if the kitchen was too small for him.

Emma ate her breakfast, wiped her sticky fingers on her overall, stroked the cat from time to time, bit into her slice of bread again and in the process dipped the fingers that had just been petting the cat into the jam. She sucked it off them with relish. Max shuddered.

'Maybe we ought to fetch a doctor after all. You're shaking.'

'Please, no doctor. No one, I don't want to . . .' He didn't finish his sentence.

He doesn't want to be caught, thought Emma. After all, he's

a thief on the run. Now he'll have to stay here. Wonderful. Such lovely eyes.

'Aren't you hungry? Have some coffee?' said Emma in dulcet tones, trying to find some way to please the man. Good heavens, why wasn't he happy? After all, he had everything: breakfast, clothes, even his life! He owed it all to her, and still he wasn't happy.

Emma waved the coffee pot his way, but he didn't react. Sat there hunched up as if he were in a cage, and finally asked, with some hesitation, 'Who left all . . . all these things lying around?'

'What things?'

'The rubbish.'

Emma scrutinized her kitchen. She couldn't see any rubbish.

'Is there rubbish lying around somewhere?' she asked, unbothered.

His eyes wandered over the room she called the kitchen. Everything that normally lives put away in cupboards was standing outside them. Everything was open instead of shut. Everything was lying about the place. Had tipped over, was flowing out, drying up, crumbling, dripping, sticking, stinking, growing mould or decaying. How long had it taken her to get the place into such a state? Not weeks or months. It must be years – she'd spent her whole life getting it this way. He guessed she was about thirty, perhaps a little older. All that time, then.

What kind of person wouldn't suffer at the sight of it? Could sit here eating instead of throwing up? He looked at her inquiringly.

Emma felt uncomfortable. She rose from the table.

'Well, too bad if you don't like it. Nothing I can do about that,' she said, and went out into the yard.

And now Max recognized the picture. He'd seen the same kitchen before, the same woman as the one just going out of the doorway. The accident was no coincidence. From the first his soul had known where it would end up. Here. With this filthy woman. So that was the cause of his nightmares and his hatred of dirt. It was nothing but the fear of death. When chaos reigned, death would come and take him away.

She'd rescued him last night, oh God, and undressed him! She'd seen everything about him. How had she got him upstairs into that bed? Carried him? How could she have done that on her own? There must be a man about this place too.

Max looked through the window at Emma, who was chasing a chicken. She was cackling like the fowl, imitating its gait.

Then she paid a visit to the dog in his kennel. Crawled towards him on all fours, barked with him, romped with him. And finally, when a pig came trotting up to her, she kissed it right on the end of its wet, dirty nose.

Now she turned to look at Max, who was sitting on the other side of the kitchen window staring at her. She knew he'd been watching her. And Emma laughed in his face, laughed and laughed.

*H*enner unwrapped his liver-sausage sandwich, although Emma and her moped were keeping him waiting. What was the matter? Why wasn't she riding it today? Had the threat of the auction sale spoiled her fun? The answer came promptly when Karl the chief fire officer drove up in the huge red fire engine with the crane on it and appeared in the tiny office of the police station.

Karl was an imposing figure. He looked like Kaiser Wilhelm minus the beard, but with the bald patch and the paunch. He himself would have claimed that the protuberance just below his chest was all muscle.

There'd been an accident on Emma's farm, he said, a car had burned out, the wreck had to be investigated and taken away.

Henner was surprised. He got into his uniform jacket, put his police cap on, and asked as they went out, 'How'd you hear? I don't know anything about it.'

'Same as usual.'

'Did anything happen to Emma?'

'Nope.'

'How come there was a car on fire in her farmyard?'

'Fell down the slope off of the main road. Forester spotted

it first thing this morning. Brought a few little trees down with it.'

'You sure nothing happened to Emma?'

Karl frowned, looked sternly at Henner and said, 'Why don't you marry her and be done with it, you fool?'

'All very well for you to talk,' said Henner gloomily.

The reason for his gloom was sitting in the back of his car, smoking and waiting for him to drive off.

Henner got into the police car. Karl followed with the fire engine and the crane. Unnecessarily, Henner switched his siren on, and, not to be outdone, Karl too switched on all his blue lights and screeching horns. Just like little boys, they drove proudly through the village making a mighty din.

Something happening at last! All the villagers came out into the street to gape, the children cheered, and Henner's mum waved happily from the back seat, greeting the people like a queen.

At the same time, a few kilometres away, Hans too was searching the road. Overnight he had come to the conclusion that Max must have had an accident. His anxiety about not just Max but also the money and the Ferrari kept him awake. He began his search at first light of dawn. Starting where he had last seen Max's car, he carefully checked every stretch of the asphalt, but he found neither braking marks nor any parts of a wrecked car – nothing. If Henner and Karl hadn't been kicking up such a racket he'd never have found Max. As it was, Hans followed the signal. Stopped, listened again, and finally found the freshly broken branches above the slope leading to Emma's farm. The sirens down below fell silent.

Hans climbed a little way down, far enough to see the police car and the fire engine that had driven into the farmyard . . . and the burned-out heap of metal. He was ashamed to find that he thought first of the Ferrari, now a total write-off, and only then of his friend's life. No, Max couldn't die, he was much too young to die. As young as Hans himself, anyway. And Hans knew he wouldn't be dying for a long time yet. He didn't have the time for it – success was waiting just around the corner.

Hans hid behind the trunk of an old oak tree. Where was the bastard? Surely not dead after all? He was so angry that he was going to murder him, but Max wasn't dead. Max? No, no, not Max.

How come the car burned out? Cars burned out only in bad movies. It had fallen down the slope, that was all. And in the rain last night, too. There was something fishy here!

He watched what was going on down below: a small policeman got out of the police car. An old lady smoking a cigarette tried to follow him, but was sent back inside the car. A sturdy fireman arrived. And a woman who looked like a farmer.

Unobserved by anyone, Max had been crouching beside the stream further up, cleaning his shoes in the water. When the vehicles arrived he took flight. He hid on the veranda of the sauna, as only Emma noticed. That was the final proof that Max was in trouble of some kind, or in any case was keeping well out of the way of the police.

You wait, my lad, she thought, smiling, and went over to Henner and Karl as they got out of the car and the fire engine. Now she'd get her own back on him for thinking of her kitchen as a rubbish heap.

'Hello, Henner dear, lovely day, Karl.'

Henner scratched his head. What was this all in aid of?

Emma's voice was sweet as pan pipes. 'Good morning, Mother Schulze. How's your bile doing today?'

Karl cast Henner an inquiring glance. It said: What's up with her, then? Henner just shrugged. Once again, he had no idea. And as Henner and Karl asked about the accident, Emma, for some strange reason, was walking backwards, getting closer and closer to the bathhouse. Luring the men after her.

Had she seen anything in the night? When did the car fall down the slope? How did it come to catch fire? But Emma had heard nothing, seen nothing. The driver? No, there was no sign of one here.

Thankful and relieved, Max heard her shielding him. But she was still coming closer. Soon the two men would be able to see him here on the veranda. Why was she doing it?

Max found himself forced to push the wooden door of the hot sauna open and hide behind it. It wasn't closed yet. But the three were coming still closer. Max was caught in a trap. He had no option: he must plunge into the heat and shut the door after him.

Emma heard it slam, and smiled with inward glee. She was now standing with the two uniformed men right outside the bathhouse. Talking about one thing, thinking about another.

Inside, Max stripped off his clothes. First his shirt, then his trousers and shoes. He was entirely surrounded by steam, sweating and trembling with fear at the same time.

Emma let him stew, and with Henner's help even put more wood on the fire.

Meanwhile Karl was investigating the charred wreck, but he found no corpse in it. The driver had vanished without a trace. He sniffed around the burned-out car, inspected the paint on the roof, the underside, the engine compartment. And beckoned Henner over.

'Listen, the roof is burned off and all rusty, but there's intact areas of paint underneath. The whole thing stinks of petrol. That fire never started in the engine.'

'Someone did it on purpose?' Henner worked out.

Karl nodded. 'For sure.'

'Why would the driver have set fire to the car after the accident?'

'Or Emma,' said Karl.

'You think Emma . . . ? What for?'

Karl shrugged his shoulders.

Henner gave him the go-ahead to take the car away for salvage.

Hans was standing too far off. He listened, hidden behind the oak, but he couldn't hear a thing. However, he worked it out that, if they'd found a dead driver, the CID from town would have been called in. So Max was alive, thank God! And the money? Why had he set the car on fire? It meant he still had the money. The crane took forever to get the remains of that beautiful Ferrari on board. It broke Hans's heart. Just let Max wait till he got his hands on him!

Max, meanwhile, was lying on the floor of the hot sauna, gasping for air through the crack at the doorway.

Karl and Henner opened the doors of their vehicles, about to set off. Fresh hope revived in Max, who felt he was almost cooked by now. Then Emma asked if the two men would like a cup of tea!

Tea? thought Max.

Tea? Henner and Karl asked themselves. Emma had never in her life made tea, let alone drunk it.

Only Henner's mother stirred on the back seat of the police car, making a move to get out and calling, 'Tea? Oh yes, I'll have a cup of tea.'

Henner was really worried about Emma. Tea? She urgently needed a good rest, or she'd go right to pieces.

'Nothing doing,' said Henner crossly, 'you're not having any tea.' And he firmly forced his mother into the back seat again.

'But I want tea!'

'That's enough of that.'

Karl nodded appreciatively.

Henner got into the car and drove away, and Karl followed him with the fire engine and the crane.

Hans suddenly noticed a steaming something running out of the bathhouse like lightning in the direction of the stream. A stark naked, red something that sprang into the water with a great leap, screeching. As it went in, the water hissed. Emma began dancing with delight. She rolled over on the ground and shouted for joy. The dog came running along, barking, chickens fluttered up.

Hans recognized Max. So he was here! What on earth did all

this mean? Hans couldn't make any sense of it. He'd think about it tonight. He quickly climbed the slope again. Max in a sauna? In a muddy stream? Max stealing from his friend and writing off a Ferrari? Hans had thought he knew Max well. But obviously he'd been mistaken.

By now Max had cooled off. He was sitting in a stream that ran straight from its source in the forest. He was very clean, but very cold too. And he was naked and dared not get out of the stream, because Emma was standing there grinning and gaping at him. He was smiling. And at last he was friendlier to her. So the sauna had worked after all.

'My name's Max, by the way.'

'And mine's Emma.'

'Pleased to meet you,' said Max.

'You're welcome,' said Emma. 'Pleased to meet you too.'

'Thanks for not giving me away.'

'Looks like you're in trouble?'

'Kind of, yes.'

'Never mind.'

'Thanks.'

'Don't mention it.'

'Lovely sauna, all the same.'

'Oh, isn't it? Very healthy too.'

'Is that so?'

Max's skin had gone red in the sauna. Now it was rapidly turning blue. Max began to shake. His teeth were chattering. Emma finally left him in peace and went back into the house.

67

On the way the rooster met her. His usual announcement, 'Nothing special to report,' wasn't going to fill the bill today.

'Permission to report: car, accident, strange man, fire. Doodle-do?'

The rooster had been thrown out of his usual routine. Emma bent down and stroked his comb.

'Don't you worry, the man can't crow.'

'It was always just fine without him. He's no good to you,' complained the rooster.

Emma smiled. 'Oh yes, he is, it will be fine with him here too.'

'Humans are bad.'

'Not him.'

She walked away and back to the house. The rooster's comb swelled with jealousy.

Max got out of the water and ran back through the warm air to the bathhouse, where he found some sheet-sized lengths of linen. He wrapped himself up in them and lay in the hammock on the veranda. It was almost like his Mexican island.

A wonderful feeling. First so hot, then so cold, now so warm. A really good feeling. He could get used to this. The sun was shining, the sky was blue, a lark sang. Suddenly his troubles seemed far, far away. Time had stopped, his thoughts weren't straying to the past or the dark future, they'd come to a halt just where they were. He had discovered the pleasures of the moment; for the first time ever he was living in the present.

*E*mma's birth had been a disaster for the pig farm. Her mother had waited before finally getting pregnant. Her female insides were not in a good way, and she could have only one child. It was a girl. That meant the family name would die out and the farm be ruined. It all came to an end with Emma.

Her grandfather blamed his son, who failed at everything he did, couldn't even father a proper son and heir.

But Emma grew and thrived, was hungry, healthy and full of curiosity. Secretly, her father was proud of his daughter.

The little girl lent him a hand whenever she could. She cut her hair short, ran around getting grubby all the time, wore trousers rather than skirts, climbed higher up trees than any of the boys she knew. She never played with dolls. At the age of seven she could already drive the tractor, and she worked like a horse. All the same, her father regularly and bitterly said, 'Oh, if only you were a boy!'

That remark crushed all Emma's hopes. She had done all she could to make him proud of her. But her sex was something she couldn't change. When Emma's breasts grew, her father stopped talking to her.

Her grandfather treated her in two different ways. On the one hand he despised her, on the other hand he trained her as if she were a grandson.

Every spring he showed Emma what she risked if she acted like a girl. If she shouted for help, if she showed her soft side. If she didn't work like all the others here, feeding and slaughtering the livestock. He intended to impress on his granddaughter once and for all what was what, show her the meaning of her life. He did it with sparrows.

As soon as the weather began to get warm he watched for those apparently useless birds, building their nests in the gutters and stopping them up. He could just have cleared the nests away without making a big fuss of it. But Emma's grandfather wasn't bothered about keeping the drains clear so much as teaching Emma a lesson.

She watched entranced as the sparrow parents celebrated their wedding, made love, and as the hen sparrows proudly laid their eggs. Grandfather had nothing but mockery for the way the cock sparrows carried on, considerately feeding the females so that they could brood on the eggs in peace.

Even now Grandfather had a chance to clear away the sparrows' nests without making any big deal of it. After all, they were stopping up the gutters. But he waited.

Waited until all the baby sparrows had hatched out and were cheeping hungrily for food. At this time the parent sparrows were particularly attentive to their chicks. It was a process of give and take, of anxious solicitude, and Emma's grandfather had no time for it. This idyll suited him nicely.

In a deep voice, he ordered, 'Emma, come here.'

The child was afraid of him. Was he going to beat her again? What was he going to do?

'I don't want to, Grandfather,' wailed the little girl.

His voice sounded as if he were training a dog.

'I said, come here.'

There was nothing Emma could do but obey. She saw her father, looking alarmed, hiding behind a shed door.

Grandfather put up a ladder against the house, and Emma had to hold it. The old man climbed up. The child, sensing that the sparrows were in great danger, pleaded with him. 'They haven't done anything bad, they're only little.'

But the old man reached into the nest with his huge paws, picked up all the newly hatched sparrow chicks, and climbed down the ladder again with them. The parent birds were twittering frantically, fearing for the lives of their young.

Grandfather held his fist in front of Emma's face and opened it. The tiny birds sat there in his hand, their skin bare and so thin that you could see their internal organs through it. They had broad yellow beaks.

'You just mark my words,' said Grandfather. 'These birds, they eat everything I sow and harvest with the toil of my hands. They don't sow or harvest anything themselves!'

As a small child, Emma went on wailing and begging him to spare the chicks. As a schoolgirl she tried explanations and arguments. In vain. Later she just kept quiet. Gritted her teeth and looked away.

'Here, you!'

Grandfather poked her roughly in the ribs. The cruel ritual was repeated every spring as he held the cheeping sparrows in his hand.

'Anyone that wants to live and eat on this farm, they have to work too. Get that into your head. Anyone who doesn't . . .'

His voice grew threatening, and the rest of his message was action. He took aim, swung his great paw powerfully through the air, and flung the young sparrows at the wall of the house, smashing them to pieces. Emma's body twitched. As for her grandfather, he relished the distress he had caused the child. And of course he was also getting at his adult son, who stood biting the back of his hand on the other side of the door. He had gone through the same thing himself as a little boy, and he couldn't protect his daughter from it now.

Even days later, Emma's grandfather was still chuckling nastily to himself as he conjured up the picture of little Emma's horrified face, or the look of his cowering son. Grandfather had a strong lust for power.

Dissolving into tears, Emma would look at the chicks' shattered bodies. She knew she couldn't put them together again or bring them back to life. After the ritual her features were hard and set for days, sometimes even weeks. She had panic attacks at night, she cried out and shed tears, ran frantically around the house, and could remember nothing about it next morning. It was always like that when spring came. Emma knew what was what by now.

*

In defiance of all justice, her despotic grandfather died a very peaceful death. At the venerable age of eighty-five he simply fell painlessly asleep, without ever having been sick. Emma's father, on the other hand, died in a motorbike accident. He had borrowed the bike, wanted to feel more horsepower for once than his little Zündapp could deliver. And he had been drinking.

Her father came off the road in the neighbouring village and smashed into the red church wall. His right leg was torn off his body, his eyeballs burst, and part of his brain spilled out on the village street. Emma always said he had died like a sparrow.

Only two weeks later, Emma's mother fell down dead in the kitchen. Even the doctor couldn't say what had been wrong with her. No one in Emma's part of the country was interested in what people died of.

Emma was seventeen at the time, and still hadn't started her periods. Of all times, they began at her mother's funeral. So she had first ovulated two weeks earlier, on the very day when her father rode into the church wall. Whenever she had the curse she was reminded of her parents' death. There was nothing she could do about that now.

Emma stayed at the farm by herself. She threw herself into pig-breeding, and she slaughtered the pigs herself. Those who want to eat have to work too.

And there was plenty of work to be done. It was a long time since she'd needed her grandfather to tell her that. Even without chains, Emma was bound to the farm.

*

So now she stood in her slaughterhouse, looking at the cleaned implements and sharpened knives lying there in order, ready for use. She had carefully prepared everything for pig-killing day. The spices were freshly ground, the mincer and the sausage-making machine had been cleaned and assembled.

The tools and cast-iron implements had been in the family for generations. Some of the knives dated right back to her great-grandfather's time. Her grandfather had bought the sausage-making machine, her father had bought the electric mincer.

Old Flachsmeier came to sharpen the knives four times a year. He also brought their overalls to the house on his Ape scooter, a kind of moped on three metal-rimmed wheels with a payload area at the back. A two-stroke machine that he'd brought back from Italy. Hard as it was to believe it, Flachsmeier had been there once when he was young. He was always tinkering about with his Ape, repairing it; the name is Italian and means 'bee'.

When Emma was born he'd brought the towelling nappies to the farmhouse on it. And he still came with household soap, brushes, shoelaces, boots, flypapers, cold cream, gun cartridges, coarse-weave underwear and overalls.

Flachsmeier was the last of the travelling pedlars, and his profession was as far behind the times as his mind. Around where Emma lived, everything was older than it was anywhere else. At some point time had either stopped or was running more slowly. The new millennium had begun without changing anything in the lives of Emma, the potato farmer, Henner or Flachsmeier. Henner had a police car of a kind that no other policeman drove now. The potato farmer still dug his harvest from the earth with his own hands, as in the past; Flachsmeier had his three-wheeled bee; and Emma cut the throats of her pigs as pigs' throats had been cut for thousands of years, and made sausages of them.

But today Emma looked listlessly at her implements and decided to postpone the business of butchery until the next day. It was almost twelve, too much had happened today already, she'd had enough. She didn't feel in the least like killing a pig. She went out and leaned against the door. Looked across at the bathhouse, where the strange man lay dozing. Perhaps he liked it here in the hammock now. Emma would like it if *he* liked it. Then he'd stay. She wanted so much for him to stay.

She felt an uncomfortable pressure on her eyelids. Why did her throat feel so tight? Why did her temples hurt on both sides of her head so often? Why was no work too much for her? How come she couldn't sleep until she'd been toiling away for fourteen hours, and her body felt as sore as if she'd been beaten?

Why did she do what she did? Why didn't she go away from here and do something else? She was here and did what had to be done. All by herself, every day, never taking a holiday. She didn't even go into town. Why would she? She had a moped. A house. Overalls. Pigs.

It was lucky she had the pigs.

Full of longings and new dreams, Emma went up to the straw loft. Not to the corner where she slept, but further back. She raised a heavy trapdoor in the floor of the loft. Right underneath it was the old sow's sty. The sow hadn't farrowed for a long time. Emma ought really to have slaughtered her ages ago, but she just couldn't bring herself to do it. Not this old lady.

She threw a bale of straw down through the hatch. Then she sat on the edge of the opening, let her legs dangle, and jumped down after the bale into the sow's sty. She took her penknife out of her overall pocket, cut the bale open and spread the straw around. The old sow liked that a lot. She nudged it with her damp nose, which was the shape of a power point, rooted about, snuffled, and finally rolled her huge, fat body comfortably around in the straw.

Emma copied her: rooted, snuffled, rolled around. Lay down with the sow in the straw, pressed close to her body, which was much larger than Emma's own and four or five times heavier.

A pig's skin is like human skin. The organs are similar too, and are in almost the same place in sows as in human beings. No other animal resembles humans as much as the pig.

Emma pushed closer to the animal to feel the pressure more strongly. They both enjoyed it. Animals will shrink from a light touch, but a strong slap on the back or the flank, a firm pressure reassures them.

There in the fresh straw with the fat sow, Emma could relax. She wasn't bothered by the threat of the auction sale, Henner's mother, or the dollar bills. Just now she'd been afraid the man would go away again. But here in the pigsty she felt her hopes revive: maybe he would stay. Stay for ever.

*M*ax had gone to sleep in the hammock. When he woke up he collected his clothes from the sauna, which had cooled off by now.

He examined the bathhouse rather more closely, and marvelled at the carving over the window frames. Round, regular decorative motifs reminiscent of dandelion leaves and large daisies. The carvings were painted yellow, red and pink, the window frames were green. The bathhouse looked as if it had lost its way. As if it had come from Russia on its travels and got stuck here. Max couldn't suppress a grin when he thought that he too was stuck here, because this was not by any stretch of the imagination where he belonged.

The bathhouse was beautiful, the garden was glorious. So why, wondered Max, was the house in such chaos? Why were the doors of all the sheds left open, why did the chickens run free leaving chicken shit everywhere? Why did no one keep the dung heap within bounds? He shuddered. He saw the pigs dozing in the dirt under the beech tree. Luckily a fence had been put up around the meadow or he'd have run away at once in alarm. These pigs were much larger than he'd have expected. Not that he'd ever seen a live pig before; he knew them only as pork cutlets, beaten out flat and pre-packed.

Max also ate eggs – in fact, he liked eggs. But he'd never seen a hen laying one. Emma's chickens were brown. They scratched about, they pecked, they left droppings. If one of them ventured over to the bathhouse he'd shoo it away. This was his territory now.

Max looked around in search of Emma, but she was nowhere to be seen or heard. He quietly opened the door of the big barn. It was cool and dark inside. Shafts of sunlight fell in through the dusty windows. Countless motes of dust danced in the light, glittering like tiny diamonds set in the air.

A harrow and a plough stood there. A cart, a small tractor, sacks, pesticides. There was straw in a loft above the farm buildings, with a loft ladder placed ready.

Max saw a large steel claw arm under the roof, with electric wiring leading to it and then on down to the barn door. Stout cables reached up to the straw loft. He saw all this without knowing what it was for.

He assumed that the straw was clean, and didn't notice the mice with their brown eyes fixed curiously on him. There was also an owl in the barn, and bats hanging under the roof. Max did see the finely spun spiders' webs, but luckily he didn't notice how disgustingly fat the spiders crouching in the middle of the cobwebs were. The rat who lived behind the seed potatoes would have horrified him too; it was an albino rat, and even Emma had only once set eyes on it.

Max climbed up the bales of straw and then slid down some hay bales. They smelled wonderful, a little like his bath salts at home.

Of course Emma had left the trapdoor down to the pigsty open – she couldn't have guessed he'd explore. She wasn't used to the idea that there could be someone moving around up in the loft. Max was proud of having ventured so far, proud of the fact that he didn't mind the dust too much.

Now he was standing right above the open hatch, his face hidden by a beam in the roof. The stout owl who had been sleeping on it had been woken by the intruder's movements. It innocently hooted. 'Tu-whit, tu-whoo.'

Max froze. The bird was right in front of him, twenty centimetres from his face. The shock hit him like a blow in the stomach.

He cried out.

That woke the bats. They flew up briefly and changed places. That was all, but it was a frightening sound. Max cried out again, started tottering in his alarm, lost his footing, fell through the hatch into the pigsty and landed on the old sow's back, scoring a direct hit. She squealed with pain and terror, and Max squealed too, just like a pig.

Emma reacted like lightning. She picked Max up and, exerting all her strength, threw him over the fencing around the sty into safety. Even she had good reason to feel afraid of the sow now, for an animal given such a bad fright is unpredictable. A sow was capable of killing her piglets at such a moment. Emma quickly followed Max.

He was totally confused. Emma took his hand and led him out into the open air. Max was shaking and pale with horror, Emma was out of breath.

Max's legs gave way under him and he slid to the ground. Emma knelt down beside him, laid his head in her lap, caressed and reassured him.

'You threw me over the fence!' quavered Max.

Emma grinned proudly, showed him her biceps and tensed her muscles. 'Not bad, right?'

'I want to go home,' sobbed Max.

For the first time, Emma had another human being in her lap. It had always been animals before, just animals. Henner never let anyone caress him. Happy to think she could offer protection, she stroked Max's head. She'd never known anything like this before, never felt anything like it. She wouldn't be able to give him up, never again. He was going to stay at home here. With her.

When Max had control of himself again, he wanted to go back to the bathhouse. Emma made him a bed there, with a mattress, pillows and blankets, put a candle in the bathhouse, brought him a carafe of apple juice, and left him alone. He didn't utter another sound.

Later, in the afternoon, she saw him lying in the hammock again. She picked some fruit and vegetables in her garden, cleaned them and cut them up small, a whole plateful. She placed them on the veranda table beside him. He nodded without a word, as if thanking her.

When she came back in the evening the plate and the hammock were both empty. She sat down on the veranda, and yes, here he came out of the sauna, now his bedroom. He stopped in the doorway.

Emma had brought him a torch and more candles. He must be careful, she told him, a wooden building like this easily caught fire.

Rather awkwardly, he got out what he had to say. 'Thank you very much for your hospitality, but I'm afraid I mustn't impose on it any longer. Tomorrow I have to . . . oh!'

He collapsed, writhing and crying out in pain. Emma hurried up to him, asking anxiously if he'd hurt himself in the fall from the loft. When he could get his breath back again he pushed Emma away. He didn't want to be supported. But he still stood there bent over, holding on to the door frame and groaning.

'Thanks, no . . . not the fall, nothing wrong. Only my stomach, it's an old story. It will pass over. I'll be off tomorrow morning. Thank you very much for everything. Good night.'

He gave her no chance to reply. The door was already shut again.

Emma went to her bedroom and smelled the quilt on her bed. His aroma still clung to it. An aroma of resinous wood and cinnamon. Why did the man with the lovely brown eyes want to go away again now?

A woman rescues a man for a change, instead of the other way around, comforts him like a mother, and afterwards he feels ashamed of himself? Was that why he was so silent? Where did he think he was going without any money?

There was a mirror on the left-hand door of Emma's wardrobe. She looked at herself in it this evening as she undressed. She had tied her brown hair back and pinned it up. She lost herself in her own eyes and dreamed of other hands letting her hair down. Clean, white hands on her shoulders. A man's hands slowly unbuttoning the silly overall, cradling her breasts, caressing and stimulating them, stripping the overall off her shoulders until it fell to the floor.

Her hand slipped down her belly, circled her navel, and her fingers sank into her pubic hair. She left one hand there and laid the other over her breasts. Naked like that, she went to the open window and looked at the beautiful, clear starry sky. The bathhouse was a long way off and on the other side of the house, so Max couldn't see her. If he had, the picture would have reminded him of something. Emma looked like Botticelli's Venus standing there – only the shell was missing. But to make up for that the wind was in the west.

'Dear God, what do I have to do to keep him?' she asked the sky as she stood at the window naked.

Silence.

Only the crickets chirped and the field mice scratched themselves. The wind changed. Her prayer was heartfelt, but no answer came.

Sometimes Emma felt really, really hungry, for instance when she was out in the fields turning the hay and she'd for-gotten to bring elevenses. Her hunger grew and swelled, demanded attention. At such times the proportions of her body changed. Her stomach was king, the centre of her being. Empty as it was, it grew enormous. It kept shouting, 'Fill me, eat. Please, this hurts!'

And thirst was equally demanding: when her bottle of water was empty, and sweat was stealing Emma's last drops of moisture, when her mouth cried out for liquid, her tongue felt thick and heavy. Her whole body seemed to be in danger, nothing else mattered if it could just have water. Alarm bells rang, her senses ran wild.

And now, suddenly, along came lust, acting just like hunger and thirst. This was something new to Emma. She'd always felt a little bit of lust, but now its demands were infinite. Emma felt desperate, like someone who feared for her life. And so indeed she did, but not for her own life, for a new life to make its way out of her. Emma was a healthy woman of the right age, her body cried out to be impregnated. A greedy desire had risen in her, and there was no holding it back now. She longed so much for the man to take what had fallen into his hands. To feel her breasts, put them to his lips. Lick and suck them. She wanted to feel his firm fingers sliding into her, pressing and grasping her, stroking and rubbing. She wanted him to tear off her overall, oh, to be masterful, please! And she wanted his tongue to go deep into her, to take her at last. Heavens, she'd die for that!

Oh, you, you man, who brought you to my farmyard in the night? Come and take me, do! But how could he have heard her? How could she have got through to that reserved man? How do you keep someone who wants to go away?

*E*mma put her clothes on again and ran through the dark night without any light. She didn't want to be seen, and anyway she herself knew every stone, every tree stump, every path around here. She went the few hundred metres over the meadow towards the village. Then on to the little church and past the old school. Henner lived on the outskirts of the village.

Emma woke him by whistling through her fingers.

He peered out of the dormer window, looking tired but well disposed.

'Yes?' He looked up at the dark sky and added, 'What, now?'

'Tell me, Henner. How do you play the lottery?' asked Emma.

Henner took a deep breath. So she *had* gone round the bend.

"Wait a minute, I'll open the door.'

He crept downstairs so as not to wake his mother. That was all he needed just now. He let Emma in. In the kitchen, unasked, Henner opened two bottles of beer and put them on the table. He clinked his bottle against Emma's, although she hadn't touched it yet. Henner noticed the glazed look in her eyes. She seemed to him more agitated than usual. And her voice sounded different.

'I had a kind of inspiration just now. I saw money raining down on me, lots and lots of banknotes.'

'Fancy that.'

Henner let her go on.

'But no one's going to give me anything and I can't inherit a legacy – I don't have relations to leave me one. And I wouldn't steal, would I? Would I, Henner?'

'No, you wouldn't steal. That would be theft, and theft's against the law.'

'There, you see, Henner? You taught me that. So there's only the lottery left. Right, Henner?'

'And you think you'd win?'

Now Emma did pick up her beer. She drank almost half the bottle at a single draught. Wiped her mouth and explained once again.

'I just had this inspiration. Tell me, Henner, how do you do it? The lottery, I mean.'

'Well, I can bring you a lottery ticket. They sell them at the kiosk where I always buy my liquorice sticks. Tomorrow afternoon, OK? Then I'll show you how to fill it in, and then we'll see.'

'Henner, tomorrow afternoon's too late, the inspiration says I have to do it first thing in the morning.'

'Early or late makes no difference, they don't do the draw until Saturday.'

'No, Henner, I mean because of the right numbers. Playing the lottery's no good if I pick the wrong numbers.'

'That's right, then you lose. With the wrong numbers.'

'You see, Henner? But I have to win, and I can only pick the right numbers first thing tomorrow morning. I have this kind of feeling about it. Only first thing tomorrow. That's why I came here so late, to talk to you about it.'

It sounded like some kind of silly sketch: farmhand and maid exchange rustic banter in the cowshed, that sort of thing. But first, Emma thought Henner was a simple soul at heart. And second, she had to make herself out silly so that he'd go on thinking her nerves were all on edge. Then he'd do something for her, and that was what she wanted. Emma took no interest at all in playing the lottery. She just wanted him to turn up at the farm very early tomorrow with the police car.

'What about it, Henner?' Emma finished the bottle. And perhaps it would also serve as an explanation of why she'd so suddenly come by money. A win on the lottery. Intuition.

'Well, if you say so, Emma.'

Henner gave her a furtive smile, and added more boldly, 'Darling.'

Emma, her body still crying out hungrily, began to hope she might at least get a little something. 'Am I your darling?'

Henner said, awkwardly, 'Well, sure.'

'Henner, is there anything you want from me?'

Emma sat on his lap. Fiddled with his pyjamas. But Henner shifted about on his chair and turned coy. 'Better not here, not just now.'

'So what was all that about being your darling?' asked Emma crossly.

'Only wanted to say what a darling you are. Doesn't need to put ideas into your head. Well. I just wanted to say something nice. When you're having such a bad time and all.'

'Say something nice but not do something nice, right?'

Henner's head moved back and forth as if the joints in his neck had worked loose.

'It'd wake her up, and she'd be on at me tomorrow morning. Asking why I had to go doing it and so on. I don't like that.'

Emma was frustrated. Furious! Furious with a hissing double *s*! Furiouss!

'See you first thing tomorrow, then. With a lottery ticket, right?'

Henner had to change his plans, which was very difficult to him, like anything out of the ordinary daily round. 'Then I'll go and buy my liquorice first thing. I never usually do that. Flachsmeier will wonder why I'm suddenly coming to buy my liquorice so early. And why I want a lottery ticket too. He's not used to me buying a lottery ticket.'

Emma spoke like a long-suffering hospital nurse. 'Well then, Henner, give him a surprise for once, why not?'

Henner opened the front door. It had begun to rain, and Emma hadn't brought anything to keep the rain off. Henner gave her one of his mother's huge headscarves. It looked silly, but she put it over her head, tied it under the chin, and pushed it well down over her eyes.

'You look like a witch in that.'

'Thank you very much, Henner. How kind.'

He didn't even notice her sarcasm.

'Well, thanks for the compliment,' she added, 'and thanks

88

for the lovely evening. I'm off back to my gingerbread house now. good night.'

Emma strode out more vigorously than usual as she went home. She'd got what she went for, yes – but as for anything else! And Henner saying 'darling' like that! She was furious with a double *s*. Furiouss.

The tame raven was on the path through the fields back to her farm, waiting for her.

'Hi, raven,' she said.

Emma had found the raven long ago, before he was even fledged. He had fallen out of the nest and broken a wing, and she had managed to get the wing better and rear him. Today he came and went as he liked. Emma was glad to see him. He flew up on her left shoulder and kept her company for a little way.

Emma told him about Henner being so mean, and how furious he'd made her. The raven croaked something to the effect that such conduct was frowned upon even in raven society. Sending a woman away when she was looking for love. It was a sin!

And Emma said, 'Yes, exactly, a sin and a shame.'

Meanwhile, Hans had made his way back to Emma's farm and slunk into the house. First he listened for any sounds in the darkness, maybe Max or the woman making small noises as they slept, but the place seemed to be empty. Not a living soul about. Max must be somewhere! Hans switched on his torch.

He was astonished by the untidy disorder of the downstairs rooms. He wondered what kind of car he'd be able to sell someone who lived like this. A Citroën 2CV Dolly would be too good for such an owner – its elegance would be wasted here. A Renault 4 with a manual gearshift might fill the bill, or an old Seat van with mousy grey paint. Normally he had his used cars very carefully cleaned and polished to a high gloss. With a customer as unusual as the owner of this house, he'd be more inclined to race a car down a forest path in a thunderstorm to make it the right mixture of colours.

An ancient Zündapp was leaning against the wall of the house, a model with a curved windscreen, a long time since those had been around. He'd take that in part-exchange – it could be done up for the old-timers' market. At this point his torch flickered, faded, and finally went out. The battery. Hans cursed.

Finally he tried the outhouses. He found a small oil lamp hanging from a beam on a rusty nail and lit it. There were a few more rooms tucked well out of the way behind the animals' sheds. Hans was fascinated by the treasures they contained. Farm implements like antiques, greased for storage and therefore in good condition. Ancient oak beams. Architects who restored houses would like those. He found old chairs and a magnificent table under sacks of fertilizer. And some wonderful cupboards. This farm hadn't yet been cleaned out by the dealers who went around these parts years ago, buying up everything of value that the local farmers owned. It was clear that Hans had made a tremendous discovery.

But the more he saw of the farm the less he could imagine

his friend hiding out in such a place. Meticulously clean and tidy as he was, Max would never in his life sleep in a shed or stable, let alone the filthy farmhouse itself. On the other hand, the bastard had nicked his money and wrecked his Ferrari. He'd never before have thought Max capable of such a thing. What had come over him? It was as if he'd been bewitched and replaced by a changeling overnight!

When Emma came home she could hear that the animals were restless. Had a marten got in among them? Or had Max ventured into the outhouses again after his experience with the sow? She searched the shed purposefully, and discovered the door to the rooms at the back standing open. There was even a gleam of light. Hans was scared to death by the shadow he saw appearing on the whitewashed wall: a woman in a headscarf with a raven on her shoulder.

The raven croaked.

Emma too had seen her bizarre shadow. She reacted a little faster than the strange intruder. Lowering her voice to a cackle, she instantly asked: 'Nibble, nibble, little mouse, who's been nibbling at my house?'

Hans just gaped. This couldn't be true.

'You just come here,' continued Emma, still playing the part of the wicked witch, 'come here so I can slaughter you!'

Hans pulled himself together and blinked in the faint light. 'Take it easy, old lady. I don't mean you any harm. I'm just looking for something.'

He couldn't see her face clearly. It was too dark.

'Looking for Gretel, were you? She's already in the oven.'

Hans wasn't having some old woman make fun of him. He moved towards her. The raven took fright, flapped its black wings and hopped away.

As the bird briefly diverted Hans's attention, Emma seized her opportunity, took hold of him with a practised grip and bent his arm back until he let out a yell of pain. He didn't have a chance. She propelled him ahead of her over to the shed where she kept the seed corn, and locked him in. He wouldn't get out of there in a hurry; it was where the children of the farm had been locked up for generations when the grown-ups wanted to punish them for something. Emma hated that shed.

'Let me out of here at once! I won't hurt you. Let me out this minute!'

Emma did not reply.

'I'm looking for a friend of mine. He was down by the stream today. Max. I just want a word with him, then I'll go away.'

But Emma put the key in her overall pocket and walked off. The man shouted after her. 'Hey, if you keep me locked up here it's wrongful imprisonment. It's hostage-taking; you can get years in jail for that, years and years. Open up at once!'

Emma pretended not to hear. Once outside, she was surprised at herself. What was she up to? Keeping a man prisoner? Why had she done that just now?

Max wouldn't hear the shouting. The shed was tucked well away behind the outhouses. She'd often shouted and screamed in here as a child, and nobody had ever heard her.

He was the one who'd started all that nonsense about the

wicked witch, not Emma. He was a burglar, that was all. Henner would understand if she had to explain why she'd shut him up.

So he was a friend of Max. Unless he was lying. Was he Max's enemy?

Once again Emma fetched blankets. She didn't have another spare mattress, so she found some potato sacks that the stranger could lie on, and she brought him a bottle of beer. She wasn't a hard-hearted woman.

He shouted and raged, but she didn't react, just went out again without a word. She hadn't taken off the headscarf. She'd put it on again whenever she went in to him, keeping up the character of the witch.

Hans sat in the dark. The pitch-black dark.

OK, he said to himself. Crisis management time.

Priority One: freedom.

Priority Two: revenge. Sub-heading A: on Max.

Sub-heading B: on the madwoman.

Priority Three: . . . well, he left that open for now.

Back to freedom. How? Dagmar!

Feeling for his mobile, Hans took it out of the small holder at his belt. The display lit up when he switched it on.

The battery! He hadn't charged it last night. A mistake.

Would there be enough power left for a conversation? Maybe two? He'd have to keep them as short as possible. At least he had reception here. He found that he couldn't reach Dagmar. Better not try again because of that battery! Leave it till tomorrow.

Hans slept badly that night on his makeshift bed.

93

*T*he rooster was crowing his heart out, but this morning Emma didn't want to wake up. There he stood, proud as an army officer on his dunghill, both upset and deeply insulted. There was a lot going on these days to throw him off balance. When Emma didn't get up for another hour his feelings were really hurt. He didn't press his attentions on a single hen that day. His neglect made his harem so cross that a quarrel broke out: which of them could have put him in such a bad temper? And the ladies were so stressed out with quarrelling that none of them laid any eggs.

Emma noticed none of this; she wasn't going to milk the cow or fry eggs today. All that mattered to her at the moment was the three-act drama she had staged.

Act One

Two hours after sunrise, Henner drives up to the farm in his police VW. She knows Max is watching. She asks Henner into the house. He has brought the lottery ticket. She rapidly puts crosses against numbers one to six and gives it back to him without a word, as if she's suddenly lost all interest in it. Henner can't make her out.

When Henner says goodbye outside, Emma shakes her head

conspicuously for no obvious reason. Henner looks at her in alarm. There's something wrong with the woman. He gets into the car and drives away. Curtain.

Act Two

Emma is on her way to the bathhouse with a breakfast tray full of raw fruit and vegetables. She knocks. Says good morning. On her way she turns back, as if casually, and says, 'The police were here, really early. They're looking for someone who stole something. Roadblocks and so on everywhere. They'll be combing the countryside.'

As expected, Max pricks up his ears.

'I told the police I didn't know anything about any man. That was right, wasn't it?'

She doesn't wait for an answer. Exit Emma.

Act Three

Max comes to her in the garden with his head lowered. He says, 'There's something I ought to explain.'

'Hm?'

'The car. I stole it.'

'Yes?'

'And I stole a lot of money because I badly needed it. The money was burned. In the car.'

'Oh.'

'It's me the police are after. But don't worry, I'm not a criminal. I'm perfectly harmless.'

'Yes, I can tell that.'

A pause. A long pause. She mustn't say it – it has to come from him.

'I was going to ask,' says the man who is now on her farm, 'if by any chance I could stay here until the coast is clear again?'

'No problem.'

'Thank you, that's a huge relief. Just now I can bear anything except being in jail. Not that –I don't want that just now.'

'Well, I know, who does?'

'Thanks again.'

'You're welcome.'

His head still lowered, he goes back to the bathhouse. Whatever you do, don't move at this point – stand there perfectly calmly. Emma goes slowly around the corner where she's in the clear. Curtain.

Applause! Emma danced a jig for joy. She had him in the bag! In high good humour she fetched her moped, pushed it along the path through the fields, started the engine, stepped on the gas and raced away.

On his veranda, Max heard the sound of the moped engine. At first he was afraid it was someone looking for him. Alarmed, ready to take flight, he looked in the direction of the noise and saw Emma on her Zündapp. He watched. He didn't understand. The woman rode straight ahead, fast as an arrow, stiff as a poker . . . and then slowly back again in gently curving lines.

Max had gone down to the road to get a better view. He realised that the stretch of asphalt road began somewhere in the middle of the greenery and ended at a group of trees after about a thousand metres. He couldn't make it out.

*

Hans tried his mobile again at nine in the morning.

At last. 'Hans Hilfinger Garage. Dagmar Stadtler here. How can I help you?'

'Dagmar, listen. This is Hans.'

'Hi, Hansi. Not coming to the office today?'

'No, I—'

'See, I was going to ask, can I leave early today, go to a movie with Hasi?'

'Please, Dagmar. Please listen. It's—'

'Our wedding anniversary, see? The thirteenth, oh my God, let's hope it's not an omen.'

'DAGMAR, LISTEN TO ME.'

'I'm listening, go on, what's up?' *Beep.*

'My battery's nearly finished. Some old witch has caught me, wants to roast me. She thinks' – *beep* – 'she thinks I'm Hansel. She's locked me up.'

'Ooh, a witch, fancy that! Selling another car, right? I get it now! Wish I had your imagination.'

'No, Dagmar, I'm not making up a story this time.' *Beep.* 'I'm not selling anyone a car!' *Beep.* ' . . . Dagmar, you still there? You must get them searching for me. On a farm, do you hear? A farm on the highway, 52.5 kilometres going north. Dagmar?'

No answer.

Beep!

'DAGMAR?'

The connection was broken. All was dark around Hans again. Pitch dark. Now he filled in Priority Three: make mincemeat of Dagmar.

98

*T*he very first thing Emma had learned to do was stir blood. She felt no disgust for it and was not afraid of killing. Her mother had placed Emma's hand in the warm blood when she was only a baby. And she did it whenever they killed a pig.

Other girls learned to crochet. Emma thought crochet-work was disgusting.

When Emma was four years old, she was allowed, for the first time, to hold the bowl into which the newly slaughtered pig's blood flowed.

The pig screamed when the men came to tie it up and haul it with all their might out of the sty and into the yard by ropes. It broke loose, trying to get back to the others. Grandfather followed the animal with the bolt loaded and ready, and Emma's father finally managed to grab it. It squealed with fear, but one of the two men held it and the other shot it in the forehead, shattering its brain. The bolt stunned the pig, but it wasn't dead yet. It lay on the ground and emptied its bowels, a smelly business.

'Come here,' Emma's father told his daughter. Carrying the bowl, Emma had to go over to the place with the bad stink.

She held the bowl to the unconscious animal's neck as it lay in its excrement.

Her father plunged the big knife into the pig's throat and opened the artery. It died at last, drained of its blood. Emma had overcome any disgust, and she knew, even as a little girl, that she mustn't be frightened either. Those who don't work don't eat. She bravely held the bowl under the hole in the animal's neck. What Emma remembered most clearly were the colours: the blood was red, the last of the pig's shit brown. The pig's skin was pink and dirty while the animal was alive. When the pig was dead its skin was white. The bowl was blue enamel with little white spots. The blood flowed in until the bowl was full to the brim. It didn't flow like water coming out of the tap, it flowed jerkily as if it were being pumped out. Emma always wondered exactly when the pig was still alive and when it was dead. That point must come at some stage, but who knew just when?

The blood stopped flowing; no more came out. Emma's mother put the bowl down on the stone paving of the yard a few metres away. The blood weighed several kilos, so it was too heavy for the little girl to hold for long. Emma turned up her left sleeve and dipped her little hand right down in the blood; she didn't need her mother's instructions now. The blood was warm, and the invisible substance that caused it to coagulate was floating in it. Emma had to give it visible form and take it out so that the blood would remain liquid, to be added later to minced meat and cooked offal or made into blood sausage.

Emma spread her little hand and moved her five digits

about in the blood. Fast, not slowly. Little clots gathered around her fingers, stuck to the skin. When she felt enough of them Emma took her hand out and knocked the slimy red tissue off, dropping it on the ground. And then she dipped her hand in again, stirred, took it out once more and knocked the clotted tissue off. Until no clots formed around her fingers any more. Emma was very proud of being allowed to help with this important job, and as a reward she got the slaughtered pig's curly tail. She used to run around the village with it, along with the other children. At some point each child had the curly tail pinned to the seat of its trousers. Then that child was the pig, was teased and mocked and chased. The child had to run for its life, to escape being stabbed with the knife. And when another child was wearing the curly tail and running for its life in turn, the first could tease, mock and threaten the new pig itself.

Most fun of all was when a child managed, unnoticed, to pin the pig's tail to a grown-up. If the grown-up could take a joke it was funny. If not it could be dangerous, but rather exciting too. Emma had once ventured to pin the tail to her grandfather. He was so furious he could almost have murdered her. But the satisfaction of seeing him go around with a pig's curly tail made up for her fear.

All children who had passed a test of their courage had sausages of their own specially made. You had to let the pig's slippery intestine, cleaned and preserved in salt, pass through your lips. The farmer held one end of the intestine to your left ear and ran it along your cheek, through your lips, and so to your right ear. The child's sausage would be the length of that piece of gut when it had been stuffed with chopped, seasoned meat and tied at the ends.

Whenever a farmer killed a pig he gave every child in the village a sausage inside the gut skin that had gone through that child's lips. These personal sausages were labelled with the children's names and air-dried along with the big slicing sausages. The children could eat their sausages whenever they liked.

Max, who was rocking in the hammock, feeling tired, knew nothing about any of this. His thoughts centred on the question of whether the police or Hans would find him first. Whether and when the pain would come back. All of those would probably coincide. But what difference did it make now? While he was lying in this hammock alive, everything was all right.

The rooster stalked over to the bathhouse, stopped, turned his right side to Max and stared at the new man on his farm. Their glances met. The fowl turned and changed to his left-hand side, so as to inspect Max with his other eye as well.

Now he was displaying his broad and colourful chest to the newcomer. There stood the rooster, very upright, in an almost lordly pose like a guard at a checkpoint. Max got the impression that he was being asked to show his papers and his residence permit. The two of them examined each other in silence for several minutes. The rooster's comb swelled and stood erect. Then the bird shook himself and stalked away with an injured air. Max watched him go. The rooster stopped once more, briefly raised his brightly coloured tail, and defecated in Max's direction.

Emma loved every single one of her pigs. She gave them names, she petted them affectionately and at length every day. She played with them the way some people play with dogs. And the pigs loved and trusted their mistress. Ever since Emma had been in charge of the farm, she had known she didn't want to hear the pigs screaming miserably on pig-killing day any more. Year after year she had seen how desperately they tried to defend themselves, how long they spent in mortal fear as two or three strong men hauled them out of their sty on ropes to the place of slaughter. Emma didn't want the screaming, or any men yelling and pulling them along either. She killed the pigs on her own.

In men's trousers, gigantic green gumboots, and a very long white rubber apron with its black strings wrapped twice around her waist, she walked across the yard. A slaughterman's belt dangled in front of her, with a leather sheath for the knife and a whetstone.

Emma clicked her tongue softly, and the docile pig trotted after her.

Max came closer, stopped at the weeping willow beside the stream, and looked at the two of them. He both guessed and feared what was about to happen. He saw a block and tackle, a huge wooden tub and another smaller tub, with buckets and enamel bowls standing beside them. A cleaver too. Steam was coming from the slaughterhouse.

Emma sat down on the dark basalt paving stones of the yard, under the block and tackle. The pig stood beside her. She stroked the animal's long back from head to tail, again and again. Stroked it firmly, patted it, talked to it. Max couldn't make out the words. He went a few steps closer to get a better view. The pig had gone down on the ground beside Emma like a dog. Carefully, Emma tied its hind legs with a leather strap and fixed the strap to a steel hook set in the ground.

She held the pig's forelegs firmly with her right arm, went on talking to it, kissed it on the forehead right where the men used to drive the bolt into the animal's brain.

Max ventured a little closer still. He had a feeling that he ought to help her, but how? What was she planning? She couldn't do a thing like this on her own!

The pig still lay there quietly, never making a sound. As Emma went on talking gently to the animal, she turned it over on its back. Now everything happened very fast: Emma drew out the long, sharp knife and unhesitatingly cut the pig's throat with a single, precise movement. Blood spurted, the pig lay there perfectly still, but Emma went on holding it by the legs. She began counting out loud.

'One, two, three, four, five, six, seven, eight.'

The animal's breathing was slowing down, was shallower now. Blood streamed rhythmically from the incision, fell on the paving stones and flowed away. The pig looked at Emma, wide-eyed. Now it did move as its muscles convulsed.

Max was very close to Emma by this time. He heard her speaking softly, lovingly, to the animal.

'Dear little piggy, dear little sister, thank you for keeping me company. I've loved you so much, so much. It doesn't hurt, you see. I promised you it wouldn't hurt. Goodbye, little piggy, goodbye.'

Gradually the stream of blood slowed down, and the pig slowly, quietly, let its life drain away, held safely and firmly in Emma's arms.

Max watched, bewildered and trembling all over. Emma took no notice of him. She stood up, exhausted, and went to a basin full of warm water. She washed her hands. Washed the blood off. Washed the knife too and put it aside. Dried her hands, tipped the water over her bloodstained apron, took a hose and hosed down the paving stones. The dead animal lay there motionless with a gaping wound in its throat.

Max whispered, 'I've never seen anything like that before.'

He had really meant to say he'd never seen such a strong woman as Emma before. Ever.

Silently, she went into the garden and picked an apple. She fetched the knife and held it in front of Max, blade upwards. Then she let the apple drop on the knife – and it fell swiftly and smoothly to the ground in two halves.

'I mustn't put any pressure on the knife. It has to glide easily through the neck. Are you interested to know why I do it like that?'

Max nodded.

'What's worst for animals is the fear of death, not death itself.'

Max asked, 'You mean death isn't so bad?'

'Not if someone holds them firmly. Not if you cut their throats quickly, in the right way. It's like dying in the wild. For instance, when a wolf tears a sheep to pieces. Hormones released in the dying animal act like an anaesthetic. They're as strong as morphine, so the animal dies painlessly.'

'Who says so?'

'The Beard-Man told me. A kind of hermit who used to live around here. He never ate meat himself, but he explained that to me.'

'What about before? The fear before they die?'

'My pigs know me. They don't guess anything bad might happen. They follow me, they trust me. I use their trust.'

'Use it? They trust you and you kill them.'

'Pigs are there to be killed. They live a good life so that they'll be healthy when they die and make good sausages. They live without anything to worry about, and here they even have a happy death.'

'What death is happy?'

Emma looked at Max, caught his eye, held his gaze with her own and said, 'Death at my hands.'

Max looked at the dead pig again and made no comment.

'I ought to offer to help you, but there's nothing I can do. I can't do it.'

'I know. I'll manage on my own, I always do.'

'May I watch?'

Emma shrugged one shoulder, as if it didn't matter to her. 'If you want to.'

*

Feeling weak at the knees, Max sat down on the small flight of stone steps outside the house. He didn't feel well, he had stomach cramps. He did not know if it was his illness or the scene of slaughter he had just witnessed.

The baker's and potato farmer's children came running along. Emma cut off the pig's curly tail and gave it to them. They played with it, chasing around the farmyard.

The sight made Max melancholy. He himself had never shouted so cheerfully and exuberantly. He'd usually been on his own with his parents. They had been wonderfully thoughtful, but they'd never shouted in delight or uttered happy cries. The joy of life had been knocked out of Max's parents when they were children themselves. Their childish exuberance had been stifled in the hail of bombs. They had suffered hunger and cold in the years after the bombing. They'd always been good parents to Max until he grew up. But then they simply ran out of strength and died, just like that. Together.

Max was weeping. Again! What were all these tears in aid of? He didn't want her to see him in tears, so he stood up and walked through the fields, past the ripe wheat.

In these hours here at Emma's house he had lived and felt more intensely than ever before in his whole life. Red poppies grew at the side of the field, blue cornflowers, grasses. There was a rich fragrance in the air, the sun warmed him. His hand brushed through the ears of wheat.

The Beard-Man wore only undyed clothes of linen he had woven himself, and let his hair and beard grow long. Hence his name.

He had built himself a hut above flowing water because he needed the current under him. At the time Emma was too young to understand all this. But the Beard-Man interested her a great deal, because he was so different from everyone else.

He walked through the fields picking anything he could find growing on trees and bushes. He went into people's gardens too in search of the food he needed. If anyone tried to stop him, he said: 'Behold the fowls of the air: for they sow not, neither do they reap, nor gather into barns; yet your heavenly Father feedeth them.' He did not regard taking things to eat as wrong.

Sometimes the Beard-Man came to the pig farm to chop wood. He was paid in Camembert cheese that Emma's mother had to buy specially for him. Two whole boxes of Camembert! He unwrapped them when he stopped for a rest and ate the cheese without any bread. Emma sat up in the chestnut tree, wide-eyed, watching him. It was an extraordinary sight, for you never ate cheese on a pig farm, let alone cheese without bread. Only the Beard-Man would do a thing like that. Of course he didn't drink beer or fizzy pop. Just water.

One day someone came along from an office somewhere and told him he couldn't keep his hut there above the flowing water; there was some kind of law that didn't allow it. The argument went back and forth. Then Uncle Karl drove up with the crane on the fire engine to move the hut. Everyone came to watch.

The Beard-Man stayed put in the hut as the crane picked them up. Someone or other said he could hear the Beard-Man singing. Someone else said he was praying. Yet a third claimed that he was shouting. The hut was put down again only fifty metres from the stream. The Beard-Man could have stayed there, because no harm had come to his hut. But from then on he chopped no more wood, stole no more fruit, ate no more Camembert. And a few weeks later he died. People said it was because he didn't have running water under him any more. Uncle Karl blamed himself.

'No blood,' the Beard-Man had told Emma. Blood must go into the ground, must seep away in it. It was not to be drunk, not to be eaten. No blood.

As a child she had fallen off the steps into the rosebed in midsummer one day when he was chopping wood. She shrieked, she cried out that she was bleeding. No one took any notice because they were all out in the fields. So the Beard-Man came to her aid.

There were several thorns in her little hand, and he tried to get them out as she sat on his lap, kicking and howling with pain.

The Beard-Man moistened her hand with his spit, softened up the place with his thick lips. They were warm. He didn't say a word. But as he licked her hand and removed the thorns that way, he looked closely at the pattern on its palm, which was almost exactly the same as his own: their lifelines, their heart-lines, their lines of destiny, their mounds and dells and creases, their circles and loops. His hand was old and strongly marked, hers young. But so astonishingly alike!

He looked into Emma's eyes for the first time. A moment ago she had been just a nameless little girl, a farmer's child. Now he spoke to her.

'What's your name?'

Emma said nothing.

'How old are you?'

No reply.

'Are you going to school yet?'

Shyly, Emma nodded.

'Do you ever say anything?'

Still no reply.

'What's your favourite word?'

'Word.'

At that the Beard-Man smiled. Held her hand. The thorns were gone, the child had stopped crying.

'We're like each other.'

He put his hand and hers side by side and showed her the lines and mounds, the loops and curves. Emma heard him say words she had never heard before. Even the sound was different. No one had ever spoken to her like that, all anyone said to her was: do this, don't do that, hold your tongue, not now.

Thousands of words came out of the Beard-Man's mouth, soft, sweet, sad words. And he had books.

There were words in the books like *dark*, *moon*, *animals*, *swing*, *children*, *names*. Words she hadn't seen or heard before. Where are the children? Will they come here some time? No. Where are they? In the book? No, further away. Beyond the mountains, beyond the town. The world went on and on there, he said. Emma didn't believe him.

Then, once, Emma was in one of his books. He was reading aloud about Emma.

She glowed with happiness and pride. If she was in the book, then there were two Emmas. One Emma stayed here on the farm, but the other Emma, Emma in the book, was some-where else!

The Beard-Man had written a little poem about Emma, and she beamed with delight. She hung on his lips as he read. Her own words followed at the same time. The little girl in the chestnut tree, the child he had thought mute, became a child with language.

Emma spoke as he did. She was his child in this world, his daughter of destiny. Every day he looked at the palm of her hand, and never ceased to marvel at it. Her hands were strong, muscular. The ball of her thumb curved, the indentation at the side of the hand was so deep that it almost passed over her wrist. At the same time she had a powerful thumb and fore-finger.

'You are very strong. One day you will do something impor-tant, not just think about it.'

Her lifeline divided, and he concluded, 'And you will go away some time. Far away from here, for ever. Like me.'

So Emma became a stranger to her family. Spoke differ-ently, thought differently. Read books.

When the Beard-Man died, it silenced her. But after that every clod of earth was as close to her as a friend, stones made life easier for her. The animals spoke to her, and plants grew and flowered for all they were worth, just for her.

*E*mma inserted her sharp knife between the sinew and bone of the pig's hind legs, making two holes through which she passed the crooked stick. The crooked stick looked like a clothes hanger, but it was much longer and stouter and had metal hooks at both ends. With the help of the block and tackle, she could lift the pig on the stick and later hang the carcase up. Emma skilfully moved the heavy body over to the wooden tub and let it down there.

She scalded the pig with boiling water, and then scraped the bristles and outer layer off the softened skin. She used a sharp, rounded, metal bell scraper. It was like exerting all your strength to shave a giant's stubble. She kept pouring more hot water over the pig and scraping away. There was a smell of dead skin, intensified by the hot water. Even if you killed a pig a week, as Emma did, the stench was always just as bad every time. Finally Emma had to scrape over the animal's teats and tear them off, and whenever she did that it hurt her too. As a child, the worst part of it for her had been when the men tore the pig's teats off. She would press her hands to her own little breasts and hide them. She was afraid the men would scrape her flat too some day.

Finally she removed the trotters from the pig's feet with a hook at the sharp end of her scraper. When the animal was smooth and clean, she used the block and tackle to hang the heavy body head down on the crooked stick from a broad wooden ladder, belly facing forward. And she kept on and on pouring more hot water over the carcase. Finally she let it drain.

When this part of the work was done, Emma sat down on the edge of the wooden tub, feeling weak with exhaustion and breathing heavily. The tub contained water full of bristles and scraps of skin. This was dirty work, work for men. Work that would have tired out two men at once.

Max brought her a cool beer. He gave himself one too. He would have liked to sit down beside her, but the stench was a thousand times worse for him than for her. The contents of the tub looked to him like corpse soup. He asked Emma to come and sit on the stone steps with him.

There they drank to each other. Emma was amazed. He had actually ventured into the kitchen to reach her fridge. As if casually, she asked, 'How come you stole money from your friend?'

'There was a reason, but I can't talk about it. The day before yesterday I still thought I needed the money very urgently.'

'And now?'

'Not any more.'

'Why not?'

'I wanted to have a hammock in the most beautiful place in the world. Now I do.'

He smiled and pointed at the bathhouse with his beer bottle.

'Why would you think this is the most beautiful place in the world?' asked Emma in surprise. It was the only place she knew.

'Oh, no special reason.' Max left the question open.

'So you don't need the money now?'

'No. But my friend does. I'd give it back to him, but it's burned.'

Emma nodded.

She needed the money herself to keep what, to her, was the only place in the world, beautiful or not. She had to keep it.

Her beer bottle was empty, and she went back to work.

Max watched her cut the pig's head off and then open up the belly with a short, strong incision, cutting from the pig's anus up to the first teats. She mustn't cut too far, or the entire contents of the belly would fall out at once and land on the dirty ground.

Emma pressed a tub against the pig's belly, holding it in place with her body. With one hand she cut the intestines, leaving the other hand free to lift out first the large intestine, then the small one. She cut away, staggering slightly and keeping the tub balanced with only her lower body. The work was far too hard for one person.

Max saw her stagger for the second time, and at last he went over to her. He held the tub in both hands so that the intestines could drop into it. Then they carried the receptacle away together. It contained many metres of intestine full of pig shit.

'Thanks,' she said.

He retched. Sour acid rose and burned his throat. He quickly retreated to his steps again.

Using a small cleaver, Emma hacked the pig's ribcage open, carefully took out the lungs, and placed them in water. She treated organ after organ in the same way. Max watched it all closely. Finally he felt such curiosity that he brought himself to go closer. At first he held his nose, then he ventured to take a look inside the animal now that it was opened up. He got her to show it to him and explain everything: what the stomach looked like, the kidneys, the spleen, the liver, the gall bladder.

'And where's the pancreas?' he asked.

'Oh,' said Emma, hesitating. 'I'll have to look for that. I think it lies behind the stomach. Or is it near the spleen? It's very small, looks like a squashed pear, if you see what I mean. Here, I think this is it.'

Max saw a small piece of tissue.

'Why are you interested in the pancreas, anyway?'

'Oh, no special reason.'

Emma grinned. This seemed to be a habit of his. When he said 'Oh, no special reason,' he meant, 'I'm not telling you.'

Now she cut the heart out of the pig's left side. It was still warm. The tubes of the veins and arteries stuck out on all sides of it, with a little blood still dripping from them.

Emma held the heart out to Max. Fascinated, he looked at the firm, red organ. He had never seen such a thing before. Emma explained where the blood went in and came out of it. Cut it open, showed him the valves, the ventricles, the muscle.

'It's like a human heart – ours look just the same. About the same size too. Human hearts are the size of a fist with the thumb hidden inside it.'

Emma clenched her bloodstained right hand into a fist. Max did the same with his left hand.

'Really? My own heart is that big, right?'

'Yes, of course. Mine is smaller than yours.'

Emma handed him the bleeding piece of pig's heart, still warm. 'Like to have it?'

He vigorously shook his head.

Emma took him by surprise, dipped her forefinger right inside the pig's heart where the blood was still moist. She smiled at him and smeared a little blood on his shirt, just above his heart. She had got him dirty! In alarm, he looked at her. But she had already turned to put the heart in the bowl with the other organs.

Max was smeared with blood, and smiling.

Emma gutted the entire pig, cleaned its organs, and emptied its intestines and bladder very thoroughly. She washed the parts like items of laundry, rubbing them inside and out. Then she put the intestines in salt, covered them, and placed them in the slaughterhouse, where it was cool.

She felt as if she were on stage in a theatre. She liked it when her audience shook with disgust, or when he showed amazement at her skill, her knowledge, her movements. She turned provocatively to him as she blew up the pig's bladder like a balloon and tied it at the top.

'Yuk,' he said, as she had expected. And he added, jokingly, 'What will it be in its next life, then? A football, a handball?'

'Brawn,' said Emma, laughing. 'I'll be filling it with brawn.'

And she chattered on cheerfully about her vet, and how he'd recently had an operation in town. A transplant. He'd been given a new bladder.

'And where do you think it came from? A pig!'

Emma thought the idea of a vet with a pig's bladder very funny. Chuckling, she used her large cleaver to chop the gutted pig in half along the back, cutting through the bones.

A second beer had made Max even braver. He took the heavy cleaver from her and went on chopping himself. First hesitantly, then finding the right notch with more and more confidence.

Emma praised his strength. Max knew she was lying. After a few blows he went back to his bathhouse, exhausted. But all the same, he had helped to kill a pig!

When Max had gone, Emma slipped into the boar's sty and took the bag of money out from under the straw, looked at the dollar bills, leafed through them. She stuffed them back in the bag and took them away with her. Crossed the farmyard with them and took the bag into the slaughterhouse, where she hid the bag inside her mincer.

But Emma had left a single dollar bill in the straw of the boar's sty. It was lying behind the trough, almost invisible.

*H*ans had been wrenching at the wooden boards of the shed and kicking them, but the wood was too stout to give way. He had looked for tools or cudgels among the sacks of seed corn stored there, anything to help him break the door down. There was nothing he could use. He wasn't going to be able to break his way out, so he would just have to overpower the woman when the right moment came. He waited for Emma. In the morning he had been hoping for breakfast, around midday he began to doubt whether she was going to come back at all, towards afternoon he was seized with horror at the thought of dying of hunger and thirst in here. Either she had forgotten him, as it seemed, or she was keeping him here on purpose.

All his life Hans had fancied himself as a man with a solution for every problem. Someone at his best in stressful situations. He wasn't going to let himself despair, even if panic was getting such a hold on him in this prison that he had passed from shouting abuse to bellowing and then howling.

Hans and Max had always pooled their strengths and weaknesses like an old married couple: if one of them could do something, the other wouldn't even try it. So Max was always timid, but never Hans. Max hesitated, Hans acted with decision. It meant that Max hadn't had any opportunity to take risks, while Hans allowed himself no anxieties or doubts.

When Hans heard the woman's footsteps he decided not on any account to show her he was frightened. He would be as wily as if he were making a hopeless sales pitch. At last he was recovering his old form. Hans had a new priority: fraternization with the enemy. That was how he'd do it, that was Hans as he knew himself. No cowardice for Hans!

Emma put Henner's mother's headscarf on again, pushing it down well over her forehead, when she went to Hans's dark prison with the oil lamp and a basket containing beer, sausage, fresh bread and pickled gherkins.

Hans seemed to be in a cheerful mood. 'Hello,' he said in deliberately jovial tones, while trembling with apprehension inside.

'Sorry I'm late,' Emma croaked back.

What was she going to do with this character?

'Nice farm you have here, madam.'

Emma didn't feel like playing the silly witch game any more.

'Look, I can well understand that I alarmed you last night,' he went on. 'It's a fact, I did act like a burglar breaking and entering, so if you shut me up, well, fair enough.'

Emma pushed the food in to him under the grating over his cell door, and left him the oil lamp.

'Please tell Max he has nothing to fear from me. I'm not going to blame him at all.'

So he knew Max was here with her. How? If she didn't leave at once she'd find herself letting him out, he seemed such a nice guy. But she had to think it over first. She left the shed without another word.

The man had seen Max beside the stream, he'd said so yesterday. So he'd been watching him from some vantage point. Watching from the woods, in secret. Did that sound like a friendly thing to do?

The man would stay shut up, Emma decided.

As for Hans, he pulled himself together:

So she wasn't talking in that confused way any more. Good. He had food and drink. Good.

He needed some kind of occupation if he wasn't to lose his nerve. A spider scuttled past him. Good.

On the evening of the day of the pig-killing, Emma was in her kitchen making the dish known as *Weckewerk*, a local North Hessian speciality. No Swabian, Saxon, or native of the Hanseatic ports could have stomached it. Emma called it her mish-mash. To make it you melt large quantities of leaf fat, the fresh layers of pork lard, in a huge pan. You fry onions and bacon, add soured cream, and serve it with home-made potato dumplings.

Max, feeling well rested, decided to make himself useful again. He had enjoying chopping up a pig with a cleaver. He found a similar axe in the woodpile. Picking it up in both hands, he swung it up in the air and down again. It was a heavy axe, a sharp tool. Max placed ready-sawn discs of timber on the chopping block and brought the axe down on them. At first he missed the wood as often as not, or his blows were too weak. His strength was enough for only three or four attempts, and then he had to stop for a rest. But the longer he practised the more often he succeeded, and finally Max was genuinely chopping wood. He carried the logs to the bathhouse and stacked them up.

Then he set to work on Emma's moped. Emma will be pleased, he thought.

It was already dark, the vet with the pig's bladder inside him had inspected the carcase and given it the all-clear, when Emma pushed her Zündapp up her private road after her hard day's work. Full of happy anticipation, she stepped on the gas and revved the engine. She was up late: people went to bed early in these parts. Now the villagers, woken by the sound of the moped engine, sat upright in bed and asked themselves: at night? How come she's doing it at night now?

The potato farmer reached for his stout wife, Berta. 'Hey, little sparrow, how about it then, you and me?'

'Are you out of your mind?' she snapped back. 'This isn't Saturday night!'

Emma speeded up. Nothing happened. She leaned forward, stretched her arms out, straightened her back. Nothing. She had reached the spruce trees, she turned. Speeded up again. Still nothing.

Was it because that man was in the house that she couldn't feel the vibrations any more, or had the moped gone wrong?

Emma ventured another two test drives, there and back again, and finally had to give up.

Henner assumed a single run wasn't enough for Emma any more. As with addicts who need a higher dose from time to time. He was worried about Emma, very worried. It was time something happened. High time. He got up in the middle of the night and ran a bath. His mother appeared in the bathroom doorway, her hair tousled, lit a cigarette and asked, 'Is this Saturday or what?'

Henner did not reply. He didn't feel like explaining to her.

The baker's wife lay awake, knowing that Emma was getting no satisfaction out of her moped any more, and it was like meat and drink to her. In the delightful knowledge that she herself was a decent, married woman, she reached for the baker and they started a fourth child.

Frustrated, Emma pushed the Zündapp back to the farmyard. Furiously kicked a plastic bucket standing in her way, and hit Max with it. He was standing in the yard, and asked if it ran better now.

'What do you mean, better?' she snarled.

'I repaired it, it was vibrating so badly.'

Even in the dark Max could see the steam positively coming out of Emma's ears. She shouted hysterically, threatening him with her fist, 'If you don't put it right again at once there'll be trouble!'

And she marched off angrily.

Shaking his head, Max disappeared into the bathhouse.

He'd expected thanks, but this woman always reacted unpredictably.

Emma did what unfulfilled passion often does in women: she devoured a helping of her mish-mash containing about four thousand calories. That brought her a little relief. She gave Hans some too, and he consumed it greedily, commenting, 'This stuff must contain more cholesterol than two hundredweight of scrambled eggs. The trouble is it tastes damn good.'

'What kind of money was it that Max stole?'

Hans noticed that she didn't ask *how much* money Max had stolen, but *what kind*. So she must know something.

'Dollars. American dollars.'

'How much are dollars in euros?'

'At the moment? A dollar is worth about the same as a euro.'

'Where do you exchange that kind of thing?'

She had the money!

'At a bank. But no one had better try exchanging the money for Max now. It was stolen from a bank. Registered. Every single note.'

That was an outright lie. In fact it came from the sale of furs smuggled out by the Belarusian.

'What does "registered" mean?'

No doubt about it, she had the money!

'It means that every bank knows the numbers on the notes. Go into a bank and try to exchange them and you'd be arrested. For possession of stolen money. And then the questions would start.'

'Oh dear! So what could be done about that?'

'Well, personally I'd give the money to someone who knows

about such things. Knows what to do with it. I might get thirty cents for each dollar from an expert like that.'

'Is that all?'

'I'm afraid so. But then no one would be arrested.'

Emma was tired. 'Good night,' she said.

'Good night. You know, my name is Hans. What's yours?'

'Emma.'

'Good night, then, Emma.'

''Night, Hans.'

Fraternization Stage Two successfully concluded. Freedom in sight, he just had to keep his nerve. He was passing his time in prison by training the spider. By tomorrow it ought to be able to jump through a burning tyre.

Emma was tired to death when Henner drove into the farm-yard on private business. He wore his confirmation suit, the one he also got out for funerals. Even at fourteen he had been as short and stout as he was now. He was holding a few limp Michaelmas daisies from his front garden, and once again he made Emma a subtly phrased proposal of marriage. 'Seeing as the moped's no good any more, and you're all on your own, and anyway I've known you for ever.'

Emma was in no mood for this kind of thing, none at all. 'Henner, you're my best friend. Let's leave it at that, right?'

'But now – when your farm is going to be seized and auctioned?'

'The first man who comes along and tries to take it, I'll stick him like a pig. You know I will, Henner.'

'Your jokes aren't funny, Emma.'

She took the daisies from him. 'Thank you, Henner. For everything. Like I said, you're my best friend.'

'If you mean . . .'

'I've been making my mish-mash, want some?'

The village policeman sat down in the kitchen and greedily shovelled the mixture down.

'The way you kill a pig, all by yourself! Why don't you get someone to help, say a Polish worker?'

'I don't need anyone.'

'You know what you do is against the law, cutting their throats and that?'

Emma took his plate of mish-mash away.

'Want to write it down in your notebook, Henner? If so I'll have to clear the table or your papers will get all greasy.'

'No, no.'

Henner reached for his plate, and she put it back in front of him. Smacking his lips, he went on in casual tones.

'Somebody said there was a man around the place here on your farm.'

'I'd know if there were, wouldn't I?'

'Karl said he reckoned that car had been set on fire.'

Emma made no reply to this at all.

'What'll you do now, without your farm?'

'Like I said, Henner. Play the lottery.'

He shook his head. Well fed, he rose to his feet.

''Night, Emma. You're a wonderful woman, and your mish-mash is even better. You ever want to get married, just let me know.'

*M*ax ate raw fruit and vegetables from the garden. Drank water from the spring. Next day, when Emma, in a conciliatory mood, offered him some of the mish-mash too, and he saw the dumplings swimming in fat, he had to suppress the urge to retch again. He couldn't stand fat. His sick body rebelled against it violently. But Emma saw his involuntary impulse to retch as criticism of her cooking. Offended, she suggested he could cook himself something, but he couldn't stand the filth of her kitchen.

By now, however, he couldn't resist his hunger any more either. While she cut up the pig she had once loved, Max took her kitchen in hand.

He washed, cleaned and scrubbed everything. Threw some items away, sorted others out. The work was deeply satisfying. He was delighted when he had scoured the surface of the dining table and cleaned it until it was spotless. He sorted cans and jars: savoury stuff on one side, sweet stuff on the other. She had some wonderful preserves: pickled gherkins, sweet-sour pumpkin, zucchini, baby onions, jars of jam. Now you could even see what was inside the jars. He cleaned the windows, washed the frames, took down the yellowed old curtains.

Meanwhile Emma was cutting and chopping up the two halves of the pig carcase, feeding them into the electric mincer. She now had tubs full of ground meat seasoned with huge quantities of garlic, onions, marjoram, nutmeg, pepper and salt. She stirred and mixed it all with her strong, bare arms. Fed it into the sausage-making machine, fitted the sausage skin in place, filled the skin with sausage meat and tied the sausages off. A sausage, another sausage, and yet another.

Whatever happened, Emma had to keep that money. She looked out; there was no one to be seen. She took out the bag. The bag with the money in it. She tightly rolled up each wad of dollar bills like a cigar, wrapped it in foil, and stuffed it into the soft meat inside the sausage skin. Tied off the sausage. Examined it from the outside: nothing showed. The money had disappeared from sight entirely inside the sausage, and she had tied it at the top. No one would ever think of searching that sausage for dollar bills. Not ever. Emma rolled wad after wad of dollar bills into cigars and stuffed them inside her sausages. She hung up dozens of the sausages on the long wooden poles fixed for that purpose in the cool sausage-drying space in the ceiling. They would air-dry there in the traditional way, along with the hams.

After many hours of hard work Emma had finished processing the pig. It had taken Max the same length of time to free one room in her house of its squalor.

Wearily, Emma came out of the slaughterhouse to join Max in the kitchen. He thought that this time, at least, she would be pleased. But once again the woman reacted entirely unexpectedly. You'd have thought he had made everything dirty instead of cleaning it up.

'For God's sweet sake, I don't believe it!' she yelled like a Fury. 'First my moped, now the kitchen! What have you gone and done now? What does the place look like? Where are my things?'

Patiently, he opened the cupboard doors. It was all inside, crockery here, spices there, preserves in the pantry. Max calmly explained that he had only sorted out the good from the bad. Thrown some of it away, sorted and tidied up the rest of it. He was still preaching like a parish priest at Advent.

Emma yelled, 'Who decides what's good enough to stay? Who says what's bad and has to go? Who?'

Max raised his own voice now, quite against his usual habit. After all, he had meant well, he hadn't expected her to react like this. For the first time, Max ventured a gentle remonstrance.

'What a stupid question! The dirt has to go, of course, that's what!'

'Why? Just tell me why!'

Now Max did something he had never done before in his entire life. He actually started shouting.

'Why? Because it's disgusting to eat off dirty plates and share the cheese with mice. It's disgusting to find rat droppings on the stove or bite what you think's crispbread and find it's cockroaches.'

His whole body was shaking with the effort of it. He had to hold on to the table.

Now Emma did something *she* had never done before in her

entire life: she held her tongue. She stared at him, but bravely kept her mouth closed. Secretly she knew she was a pig about housework. A pig? Pigs are a great deal cleaner than Emma was in her kitchen. Out of doors, she had everything under control, but what about in here?

Max sensed that she was trying to make up their quarrel, and calmed down a bit himself.

'I'm your guest here, I know I'm deeply in debt to you for taking me in. I'm glad of that, because they're looking for me, and I don't want anyone to find me. But I can't just nibble carrots. I'd like to be able to cook something. I could cook something for you too – in fact I'm a very good cook. But please, for heaven's sake, let me dig a way through to the kitchen stove first. Otherwise I'll never reach it.'

Emma's voice was shaking. 'Dig a way through? You have to *dig* through my kitchen?'

Max was melting with pity now. Such a strong woman, and she was trembling.

He spoke as gently as if he were about to touch her affectionately. 'Yes, dig. Please don't be cross.'

But Emma left the room without another word.

She was in total confusion. Not because he thought she was untidy or because he'd read her a lecture. No, it was something else. Here was someone being nice to her all of a sudden. It was quite a strain. Someone doing something for her! That was unheard of.

He wanted to cook her something! Not even her mother had done that. She had cooked when she had time, and Emma had had to lie in wait for the right moment, the moment when

130

there was food on the table. They had no fixed mealtimes, not even any rough idea of mealtimes.

If she was just five minutes too late she'd have missed her moment, and the others would have eaten it all. That was life here: the strongest man ate first, then the woman of the house, finally any children. This farm, with its peaceful animals, was also home to some truly ferocious human beings who bit, hit out, hissed and devoured their food. She could never have handed herself over to their tender mercies – she'd have died.

She had always been on her own, exposed to all the storms of life alone. She had never entrusted anything to another human being, given it up, given it away. It had all been her own business and nothing to do with anyone else. Even when she grew up she assumed that was normal. If a gutter was hanging loose, Emma fixed it. If there were vermin in the bedroom, if lightning struck, thieves came or there was a fire, if swine fever ruined her, if water pipes burst, rats plagued her, a sow was in trouble giving birth to her piglet, it was always Emma's business. The responsibility had lain on her shoulders alone, and it had toughened her up.

When they were all finally dead, when Emma was free of the pressure of making sure she was safe every day, she let herself go. She let everything around her go too. Let it drop and lie where it had fallen and where danger had once lurked: in the farmhouse.

Seeing yesterday's cup lying around had reminded her that there *was* a yesterday. And there'd be a tomorrow. How else was she to feel that a week had passed if the mould on the dirty crockery didn't develop and grow in those seven days? Dirt was her calendar. The height of the stacks of old newspapers was her measure of time.

Emma surrounded herself with a soft, gentle outer skin that others called dirt, but it warmed and protected her. This disorder was her inmost being, the map of her soul. But outside there was the garden. That was unencumbered ground. She could live as she liked there. The garden showed what she really wanted life to be like. The state of the house was evidence of the side of life that she couldn't cope with.

And now this man was destroying her comfort blanket of dirt. She realised there was no room in her house for a second person, for a man. But she wanted that second person, wanted to keep him with her. In her kitchen and in her bed. She must give him space if he was to stay.

Having come to this conclusion, she went back to Max. From outside, she could see him through the clean windows. She watched, touched by the trouble she saw him taking to do something he thought she would like.

Standing in the kitchen, Max opened a bag of flour. Put the open bag on the table, took a deep breath, and finally, reluctantly, tipped it over. The white flour dusted the clean table. Now he took an egg and carelessly dropped it on the table, shell and all. Broken egg dripped off the table and on to the floor. He was trying to repair the damage. Trying to get the kitchen nice and dirty again, just for her.

Much moved, she stood in the doorway and said, 'It really did look better before.'

He looked up in surprise.

'It looks really nice in here now.'

Max's eyes were wide with surprise.

'And it would be lovely if you'd cook something for me. No one's done that for ages. Not for ages and ages.'

He smiled, came closer. She was still standing in the doorway. Max went up to her and took her hand. The left hand, the one she used to kill pigs. He kissed the back of her hand, hardly touching it.

'Supper in an hour's time, all right?'

She nodded, wiped her nose on her sleeve, and went up to her bedroom to change.

She mustn't think about it now, mustn't think about anything. It was lovely, it scared her. Scared her badly. But it was incredibly lovely too. Mustn't think, no good thinking. Other people do it too. See each other. Find their way to each other. Love each other, live together, trust each other. And sometimes they part again. Emma was so scared. She wanted it, but she hardly dared to take it. He had kissed her hand.

Don't fall into a man's arms, he'll only let you drop. You'll go all soft in his hands, and then he'll crush you. If you're little and tender, the man will turn hard and mean.

Don't get close to anyone, you'll make yourself dependent. And once you're dependent you begin begging for love. Then you'll lose your dignity and your mind.

Don't fall into any man's arms, he won't hold you.

Emma had gone slowly up to her room and undressed in front of the mirror inside her wardrobe door, lost in thought. Now she looked down at herself. She liked the look of herself naked, but she couldn't go around with nothing on. All the same, she wanted him to see more of her. Wanted to make him guess how pretty she was. But her overalls would make anyone guess there were hidden horrors under them. She needed something else to wear. What else was there in her wardrobe?

She put all the overalls on her old armchair. There were a surprising number of them. First those she had bought herself in the last fifteen years. Then she found the overalls her mother used to wear. And right at the back her grandmother's overalls too. The wardrobe was huge, and the pile of garishly patterned overalls swelled and grew. There had to be over a hundred. Flachsmeier and C & A had made a fortune out of Emma's family!

Beneath the overalls her grandmother's underwear came into view. Emma had never seen these things before. She pulled out a white petticoat with old lace at the throat. It was short, it stopped a hand's breadth above her knees, and there was lace at the hem too. The fabric was thin and let her figure show through. She was strong and muscular, but not fat. She had a good figure. She left her hair down, and it made her look years younger, almost like a girl.

Emma had to laugh. She'd never dare show herself to him like this, never! But she did look good. The petticoat was pretty, made of linen. The linen must have been woven by Grandmother herself; they used to grow flax here in her time. But Emma thought she looked too naked in it; she felt ashamed. Moodily, she put one of the old overalls on over the linen petticoat and went out of her bedroom in a bad temper.

Today she took Hans a good platter of assorted cooked meats from her day's labours, with fresh liver sausage, brawn and belly of pork. That was how he heard about the pigs and the pig killing. Impressed, he asked her to tell him more. But she put it off until the next day, saying she had washing to hang out, and her own supper was waiting.

The prisoner made a hearty meal, and gave the spider some of the liver sausage too. His chronic headaches had disappeared two days ago. Could imprisonment have been a kind of cure for him?

In-the-Dark Spa. A new therapeutic trend – you might even call it an event. A retreat, no meditation and silence, just sitting in the dark. He'd have to think about that. Maybe the idea could be marketed.

Hans hadn't made his fortune yet, he was waiting for the crucial moment, for his really big coup. It had to come some time, he felt sure of that. But when? And what would it be? He'd tried stocks and shares, and the market fell. He'd backed horses that went lame, and tried women who didn't love him. When Hans went south on holiday it rained. When he forgot to buy a lottery ticket his numbers were drawn. Hans did not see this as cause for gloom, but was a hundred per cent sure that the statistical probability of his enjoying great good luck in the near future was rising all the time.

Had the moment come now? It wasn't just the antique agricultural implements in here, he was on the track of an entirely new idea. This wasn't a case of hostage-taking, thought Hans suddenly. No, it was a turning point. A moment of destiny.

He'd have to think some more about In-the-Dark Spa. Such a total absence of Dagmar. Wonderful.

Emma put up the washing line in the garden and hung sheet after sheet on it. It was early evening, but still hot, too hot for an overall and a petticoat too. Protected by the big sheets, she took the ugly, garish overall off again. The wind cooled her skin and blew around Grandmother's thin linen petticoat. It was a fine summer's day, and her mood improved.

That was how Max found Emma. She saw him indistinctly through the sheets as he came closer. Looking down at herself, she felt ashamed. Now he was right behind the laundry she had just hung up. The washing line was high, he couldn't see anything. But then his hand appeared above it, drawing the line down a little. Unexpectedly, his head emerged. He looked at Emma. She went red as a turkey.

'I've been making ratatouille,' said Max in friendly tones. 'All right?'

She nodded. Whatever ratatouille was.

He smiled, pointed to Grandmother's petticoat.

'That looks very nice. I'll find myself a jacket in your father's wardrobe, if I may. Or we won't look right together, eating our supper. OK?'

She nodded.

Don't fall into any man's arms, he'll only drop you.

'We can eat in ten minutes' time.'

And off he went.

The money. Whatever happened she must keep it. However nice he was, she was going to keep his money.

They ate supper together like that.

He said it was a pity she just had a TV set, no stereo system, or they could have listened to music while they ate.

Emma had never eaten to musical accompaniment.

'What do you listen to with a meal, then?'

'Well, Handel would be nice.'

'Oh.'

Suddenly she felt very small. She didn't know about anyone called Handel. She felt like a stranger in her own kitchen, eating this funny food. Funny because there was nothing in it but vegetables. Pig-killing time and there was nothing sensible to eat in her house. Oh, well. He wasn't kissing hands any more either. Emma went to bed hungry. Hungry twice over.

*H*ans was very different from Max. She almost pre-
ferred him, he was more straightforward, he talked to
her nicely. He said her sausage tasted wonderful, and Emma
felt proud of that. She cut him more and more of it, and they
ate in the dark together. A piece of fresh sourdough rye bread
in one hand, a slice of sausage in the other.

'Heavenly,' said Hans, smacking his lips. The fraternization
was going full steam ahead. Hans was still a prisoner and she
had the key, there was still a grating between them, but Emma
trusted him.

When he heard what a cheap price she asked for her
sausages he shook his head. It was too low. Much too low. In
Italy, he told her, there were sausages almost as good as
Emma's that cost three times as much. As for French sausages,
full of bits of fat and gristle, yuk! Expensive too. And the
English . . . had she ever eaten English sausages? No? Well,
they added paper to them, paper to stretch the pork in the
sausage-meat, and they sometimes even worked in scraps of
fabric too. Emma shook with laughter. Hans chuckled. Of
course there was nothing of the kind in English sausages, but

he didn't like English football fans, so he'd thought that up about their sausages.

She told him about the pigs, about prices, about the state of the market. And finally she even told him about the threat of foreclosure and the auction of the farm to pay off her debts. Hans sat there in his dark prison by candlelight. He had paper and pencils in front of him, and he was working on a new business strategy for her farm.

'Your pigs run around free range, right?'

'Yes, in a meadow.'

'How many square metres available to each pig?'

'Available for what?'

'Well, for running around, for living in.'

'Um . . . er . . . hard to say. A lot. I mean, they don't live in square metres, they go from the stream to their wallow under the oak tree and then back to the sty. Like that.'

'Let's say ten square metres per pig, shall we? And a stream, a pool to wallow in, the natural life, right? Living in their own community in the sunlight? Something along those lines?'

Hans made notes and did sketches, and Emma was surprised to hear him ask such obvious questions.

'Anything else?'

'No, I'm just fond of them.'

'How fond?'

'Oh, well, I talk to them all, pet them.'

'All of them?'

'Yes.'

'How often?'

'Every day.'

'The animals get petted every day, and you talk to them?'

'Yes.'

'This is crazy. No one's going to believe me!'

Hans went on and on making notes and saying things like, 'Super! Terrific! Running about free range. Happy.'

Then he thought with great concentration, wrote two words down and drew a fat, curly line around them. *Happy pigs.*

'Go on, then what?'

'When they've put on enough weight they're slaughtered.'

'Where?'

'Here.'

'How? How exactly, please? All the details.'

And Emma told him in detail how she did it. He understood. He said it was fantastic.

'Why, is that anything special?' asked Emma.

'Of course it is, Emma. You treat your animals with respect. It's a brand new method. It's unique – it's a new concept. That's it, you've invented a new concept. Well done!'

Emma went red and muttered a thank-you. She ought to let him go now. He was talking to her like a friend. He'd praised her. Who had ever done that before? Her hand slipped into her overall pocket where the key was. Hans waited in suspense, pretending to be entirely absorbed in this new idea. Noted something down. But she let go of the key again. She dared not set Hans free.

He helped her out. 'I'm almost glad to have a chance to sit here in peace and think. Not a bad idea, being able to work undisturbed for once.'

*M*ax had attacks of terrible pain in the night. His entire stomach cavity seemed to be on fire. His legs were badly swollen and felt like heavy weights pulling him down. They were chaining him to his bed; he could hardly move. Not until the first light of dawn did he fall asleep, utterly exhausted.

The next day he felt physically better, but his thoughts were as sombre and realistic as before. He had to leave this farm, he had to leave it as fast as possible. It seemed to him that Emma was a little in love with him, and he thought love wasn't something he ought to embark on now. Only just before he . . . well, he was already half dead, he couldn't tie a woman to him at this point, arouse hopes when there was no hope left.

He couldn't eat the fatty sausage Emma offered him. Fat revolted him, but she thought he just didn't like her sausage. He could eat vegetables and salads. But not pork in any shape or form. He couldn't expect her to watch a sick man dying. He would have to go to the pain management clinic the doctor had recommended. But he didn't want to give Emma any explanation, didn't want to say any goodbyes. What was he to tell her? They hardly knew each other.

*

Emma had a discussion with Hans in the shed that day. His idea had taken shape, he'd be her manager, he said, draw up contracts. He wanted to phone the United States! Hans enthusiastically explained his great idea, all that could be made of her farm, but Emma didn't understand him. He said he could make her rich; she didn't believe him. She was sure he just wanted to get out of his prison. And she would let him out, too. But first she put in a good word for Max.

'He's here at the farm with me, and I like him so much.'

'Max with a girlfriend, now that's something new!'

'And he's very sorry the money was burned.'

'Emma,' said Hans, smiling in his best showman's manner, 'what are fifty thousand dollars?'

'You mean not a lot?'

'The two of us will soon be earning far more!'

Emma could hardly believe it. 'You're not angry with him?'

'Never mind that.'

'Then I can let you out now, can I?'

'Yes, Emma.'

Hans looked at her confidently. Emma persuaded herself that he was a friend of Max, after all, so he'd keep his word. Wouldn't he? It was a risk, and Emma didn't know how people who lived in towns thought. Hans had been very nice to her all this time. Hadn't even been angry with her for keeping him shut up for days on end. So now she took the key out of her overall pocket. Hans acted as casually as possible. He stood up and brushed the dirt off his clothes as she unlocked the door. However, no sooner was it open than he seized Emma, held his arm to her throat and pressed hard.

'Bitch!'

It was a great shock. Emma instantly regretted her decision. What had she done? How stupid of her! Of course he wanted the money!

Hans held her arm firmly and twisted it. Emma cried out with pain. Hans pushed her into the shed and locked the door. Emma stared at him, unable to utter a word. No one had grabbed her like that since she'd lived alone at the farm. She was in total confusion.

'Somewhere out there,' she heard Hans say grimly, 'there's a Belarusian mobster waiting, and he's furious with me: the Ferrari written off, the money gone. If he doesn't get that money back he's going to murder me.'

Emma tried to speak, to say she'd give him back the money hidden in the sausages, but her voice failed her.

This shed had often been her prison. When she had broken the handle off a cup that was worth nothing she'd been thrown into this cell for hours. And when their horrible neighbour sat her on his lap and she struggled. When her great-aunt came to visit and Emma didn't bob a silly curtsey, when she didn't help her mother, when she'd knocked over the milk churn, when she had simply been in a certain place or, on the other hand, had *not* been in a certain place, she'd been punished by being locked in the shed.

But she wasn't a little girl any more. Slowly, Emma got to her feet. Took a run-up and rammed the door with all the force in her muscular body. No luck.

'Open this door!' she shouted.

'I was in there for days.'

'I don't want to be here,' she wept.

'Nor did I.'

Max was saying goodbye to the farm. Leaning on a stick, he went into Emma's kitchen, into her bedroom. Stroked her bed, her overalls. He looked at room after room once more, by way of saying goodbye to Emma. And the more he tried to break away from her, the more he longed to see her. The fear of losing her had gone. Because he most certainly *was* going to lose her. She was completely crazy, but there was something so special about her.

Why, he asked himself, should he leave now when he was going to leave eventually anyway? It was only a matter of weeks.

Why was he denying himself this? He'd always denied himself everything, why do the same in death? None of it mattered now, after all. So why entertain scruples when death had none? When death was coming so unfairly soon? Life is too short for scruples.

Emma stored animal feed just past the henhouses, and he heard voices there. Emma? He opened the door, saw Hans and heard Emma.

'Hans! What are you doing here? Emma . . . ?'

Hans had intended to smash Max into the ground as soon as he set eyes on him. But even in this dim light he saw how terrible Max looked. Sick. Positively wretched. So he just asked, 'Why did you steal that money? You know perfectly well what that Belarusian—'

Max interrupted him. 'Not here. Let Emma out this minute!'

Hans took the key out of his trouser pocket. 'The money?'

'You'll get it back somehow or other.'

Hans opened the shed. Emma stared at him. He had hit her. At last her anger returned. She grabbed him by the collar.

'If you ever do a thing like that again . . . !'

He offered a conciliatory hand and assured her, 'We're quits now, OK?'

Max put his arm around Emma's shoulders and led her out of the shed. He felt her trembling.

Emma knew she ought to say she had taken the money. But then she'd lose Max. She had lied to him for too long. So she still kept quiet.

Not having seen the sun for days, Hans had to narrow his eyes when he came out into the open, a free man again.

Max wanted a word with Hans alone, so he took him over to the bathhouse veranda. There he told him that the money had been burned during the accident. Hans thought the whole story incredible.

'Why would a car catch fire just because it falls down a slope? In the rain, at that?'

'I don't have the money any more, I swear I don't.'

'Emma does.'

'No, she doesn't. It can only be burned.'

Hans knew that Emma had it.

Max offered Hans his life insurance as compensation.

'Oh, great. We just wait forty years until you pop your clogs.'

Max mumbled something about a few weeks. It was difficult to make out just what he was saying, but this time Hans was listening. He was dismayed.

'Does she know?'

'No.'

The two friends had known each other all their lives, and had never before touched one another. Now Hans affectionately patted his friend's back and gave him a bear hug. And then Max wept without restraint on Hans's shoulder.

'As bad as that? Was it the accident?'

Max shook his head. 'No, before.'

'So why the money?'

'I'd . . . I wanted to go away.'

'I'd have helped you.'

'But what if you hadn't?'

'Oh no, Max! Don't start all that again!'

Hans hugged Max again, almost lovingly.

'And don't you go kissing me either,' Max teased him with the last of his strength, and even managed a slight smile.

Turning to go, Hans made Max a present of a lie. 'Don't worry. So the money was burned, it doesn't matter.'

'Take my insurance.'

'Oh, you know me.' Hans smiled at his thoughts.

The big boar, a dangerous animal, was out in the meadow. Max went into the sty and sat down on the straw, exhausted. He would so much have liked to stay here with Emma. So why didn't he just stay? He looked down at himself, stroked himself until he was hard, and smiled shyly. Well, he wasn't too ill for that yet. Why not try it with a woman for once? He had come upon her farm by chance, he'd met a woman who was more like an animal in some ways, but who had a warmer heart than any human being he had ever known. Max saw Emma in her grandmother's white petticoat, brought himself off with that picture before his mind's eye, and fell asleep in the straw of the boar's sty.

*E*mma fetched two bottles of beer, Hans fetched his charged-up mobile. They both went into Emma's hideout in the straw and opened the barn window. Hans stretched out, feeling good, and carried on with his showman's act. He didn't do or say anything to hint at what was wrong with Max.

They celebrated freedom and reconciliation with the beers. Then Hans made a phone call in English.

'Hi, Jim, Hans here. Hans Hilfinger in Germany. Yes, right. I've got a marketing idea, extraordinary, I tell you. Yes, absolutely new. No, you never heard anything like it before.

'Listen: you eat eggs, for instance. And everyone wants eggs laid by happy hens. Birds who can walk around free on a farm enjoying the fresh air, that sort of thing. Understand?'

Emma herself didn't understand a word of it. No one on this farm had ever spoken English, nor did anyone in the village. There'd never even been a visitor here who wanted to speak English. Flachsmeier let slip a few words of Italian now and then, and waxed sentimental over them. But Emma liked listening to Hans, whatever it was he was saying.

'There's this woman here who keeps pigs. She makes sausages out of the meat from her pigs. Excellent sausages. Now listen, those pigs, they live a better life than you and me, get it? They can walk around freely, she talks to them, pets them, loves them. They're happy pigs, understand? Then she kills them, they die easily, no stress, nothing. Not like pigs at the abattoir screaming in fear. They're not afraid. You could say they live happy and die happy. Get that? You don't?'

Now Hans's voice rose, as if the man at the other end of the line was having difficulty understanding him.

'No, no, personally I don't care about pigs. But the meat from these pigs is much better than ordinary pork. Yes, that's it. So my idea is we sell pork products of all kinds made from those pigs, pigs who live so happily, and we call it, wait for it: Happy Pork. You got that, Jim? We have to get the worldwide rights for Happy Pork!'

Hans laughed, and the man in America seemed to be laughing too. Hans was all excited. He kept saying *Happy Pork* and *worldwide rights*, and laughing and laughing. Until the battery of his mobile ran down again.

He flung his arms around Emma, gave her a big hug.

'We're going to get rich, you and me, Max and Jim. Rich. Ha, ha! Stinking rich. Jim says there's a pile of money to be made out of this. A whole pile of money!'

Emma knew it was because the poor man had been shut up so long, that was all, there was nothing else to it. He was dancing about like an Indian on the warpath and shouting, 'The hell with Belarus, the hell with Ferrari. The hell with the lot of them!' Then he sat down again. 'I'll have to go home to deal with all this. I'll get everything ready, contracts drawn up and so on. OK? And when I've done that I'll come back. I just need a few . . . I need some time.'

Emma nodded, simply to calm him down. Her nerves were often on edge too, but this man? He thought of one last thing.

'And the In-the-Dark Spa project, I'll get that registered as a trademark too. We'll kill two birds with one stone! Terrr-rrific!'

Hans's car, which he had driven here days ago and just left at the roadside, had disappeared. Towed away. So he rang for a taxi to come to the stone saying 52.5 kilometres on Highway 7 going north. The woman on the taxi firm's switchboard didn't believe him.

'Where's that supposed to be? Is there a name on the door?'

'It's a kilometre-stone, madam. Nobody lives there.'

'None of our drivers have ever been where you want to be picked up, never.'

The journey was too risky for the taxi firm.

Emma said she'd never seen a taxi in these parts – she didn't even know what a taxi looked like. She'd drive him back to town herself. Her own courage alarmed her, because she'd never been to town before.

'What will we go in?' asked Hans.

Hans, connoisseur of fast cars, was chugging along at a top speed of twenty-five kilometres per hour on the hard passenger seat of an ancient tractor. The tractor jolted and swayed so much that he had to hold on tight with one hand. With the other hand he was holding the piglet that Emma had insisted on giving him as compensation for being shut up in the shed. A dear little piglet, now sitting beside him and letting the wind blow in its face.

Dagmar was standing by the glass door of that high-class outfit the Hilfinger Garage when her boss's new conquest rattled into the forecourt in her tractor, after a two-hour drive.

Dagmar had been using these last few carefree working days to study all the latest women's magazines. Now she saw a vehicle pull up on the forecourt. It was right in line with the country-house style predicted by the women's mags as the latest thing. The blue-green of the lady's shirt-dress was a contrast, but a perfectly judged one, to her yellow-and-white spotted headscarf. The model's complexion was matt, just as if it were due to pure, fresh air, her foundation was very thinly applied to enhance the natural look, and her gumboots were in the British hunting, shooting and fishing tradition. The dot on the *i* of the whole thing was Dagmar's boss, Hans. He got down from the tractor and waved, and the model drove off. Hans came towards Dagmar with a piglet in his arms.

'Ooh, you got a little piggy!' squealed Dagmar. 'A little baby piggy, so tiny! Oh, no!'

'Oh, yes.' Hans smiled. 'I've definitely got a pig.' And thinking of Max, he added sadly, more to himself than Dagmar, 'And I've had a pig of a time too.'

Dagmar wrinkled her nose. 'You pong a bit.'

This was a gross understatement, because Hans hadn't washed for days and stank to high heaven. The piglet made its own contribution.

'Well, I kind of never got around to washing, you see,' said Hans.

Weeks later, Dagmar was still wondering what exactly Hans had been doing those last few days with the lady tractor-driver and the piglet. The most shocking of delightful images flitted through her mind, her imagination roamed over hill and dale, filling her sweetest dreams with deliciously climactic ideas. Dagmar bought her Hasi a loden jacket, but it didn't help much.

On the drive to town Emma had talked and laughed, although she was secretly trembling with fright. The town, the town itself, and she, Emma, in the middle of it. But goodness, what a fuss about nothing! It was fine, the street was asphalt like her private stretch of road at home. And if you didn't know which way to go you could stop and ask. What was more, the town was nowhere as confusing as she had always feared.

Hans had given her a lovely present. He told her to stop outside a factory where they made chocolate-covered marshmallow treats and bought her a box of a hundred. Soft, fresh marshmallows that melted in your mouth. She was going to consume the whole hundred by herself. This could be the start of a career as a truly imposing Whopper!

As Emma drove away from the garage, quickly stuffing the twentieth chocolate marshmallow into her mouth, she was on a sugar high.

There were shops in town, and people. Cars. Buses. Huge road junctions that didn't scare her now.

As Emma drove over the last few junctions she hooted. She felt she wasn't afraid any more. She laughed at herself, sat up straight as she drove and reached her right arm towards the sky as if she'd just won a victory. She shouted out her delight like a temperamental Italian woman waving a flag and parading through the city centre after her football team had won. In high spirits, she threw chocolate marshmallows at passers-by, yelling with pleasure. Something was on the move. Emma was in town.

*M*ax had found the dollar bill! During his exhausted sleep he had churned up the straw near the trough. He saw the dollar bill when he opened his eyes. Only a corner of it stuck out, green leaves twining around a number right in front of him. Hans had been right.

He had to sit on the edge of the trough and think. He felt terrible. He held the bill in his hands, turning it this way and that. There was no other explanation. There were just the facts. He would rather have believed the money was burned. The illusion that this woman had been genuinely interested in him was gone.

After much thought he put the dollar bill in his trouser pocket. He hurt, particularly his stomach. Suddenly he had a bad attack of flatulence. He farted loud and long. Luckily he was alone and in a pigsty. Such a thing had never happened to him before. His legs hurt. But there was nothing for it, he had to find his money again. The money that really belonged to Hans.

Max searched the whole farm, rummaged in Emma's cupboards and drawers, looked under her mattress, in the stove. In the lavatory cistern, inside pots and behind pans, in the mincer, in the tool shed, among the sausages and hams, in milk cans and in the straw. In the sow's sty among the piglets.

Her house was a disaster. There were a thousand and one ways to hide a plastic bag here. He would never find the money, never.

It had very nearly been so good here with Emma. But the car hadn't caught fire of its own accord, she must have set it alight, the bitch. To make him think the money was burned. The cow. Had he learned to use such words from her? And learned to be angry too?

However, now his strength failed. He was only just able to drag himself to the bathhouse veranda, where he collapsed and threw up. His loud retching scared even the chickens. The rooster came stalking swiftly up. Stopped beside him and watched nervously to see what was going on.

Max threw up at one end and was simultaneously racked by diarrhoea at the other. Sometimes he clung to the railings, sometimes he leaned over them, exhausted, but his bodily fluids came out of every orifice. His tears flowed, and the strain of it sent sweat through all his pores. When the retching and the cramps died down he stayed lying bent double on the floor, in all the mess that had come out of him. Gasping for air, completely worn out.

He couldn't go away now – it was too late – he couldn't go anywhere any more. What was he to do?

Slowly, he tried to get up. He couldn't stand, so he crawled on all fours out of the mess and back into the bathhouse, where, with great difficulty, his stomach hurting all the time, he took off his shirt and trousers. He collapsed again, but in the end he managed to stand up and, with the last of his strength, strip off his soiled underpants. Then, dirty as he was, he fell into his blankets and went to sleep at once.

That was how Emma found him when she came back from town. She saw the shit and vomit on the veranda and began worrying badly about him. She wouldn't clean it up; she knew he would feel ashamed later, and she didn't want to do that to him.

Max lay on his bed without moving all evening and all through the night. Early in the morning the rooster woke everyone according to rule, and with Max, of all people, he succeeded.

Max was feeling a little stronger now, at least strong enough to wash himself and clean up the veranda. He took the bed linen off and hid it in a chest along with his dirty clothes. He didn't have the strength left to wash them yet.

Emma had seen it all from a distance, registering every movement in and around his little house.

Max was lying in his hammock again, even if he was exhausted and pale. And disappointed, still deeply disappointed. Stealing from him and pretending to be in love!

All the same, he was grateful when Emma brought him rice pudding with cinnamon and sugar. She thought he looked terribly thin.

'That's what comes of not eating meat,' she muttered crossly under her breath. She didn't speak to him directly. She didn't dare. Something had happened, but she didn't know what it was.

The warm, milky dish did his stomach good. The sugar strengthened him and the smell of cinnamon was comforting. He slept in the hammock for a couple of hours after eating it. Emma never let him out of her sight, and even the rooster stood guard. But they both kept their distance.

That evening Max filled a load into a washing machine and then hung up his things. He still wasn't speaking to Emma. He drank a great deal of water, and once he had finished the laundry he lay down in the hammock again. His legs were burning and swollen. Max thought things over. She'd have to tell him where the money was. She was the only person who knew, and she would tell him. Simple. But he'd have to think up some trick or he'd never find out. He needed a few days of rest now, and he was glad to have Emma looking after him. And glad that she didn't ask questions.

*I*n Emma's dream, globes hovered and changed shape in the air: each divided, became two or three globes and then merged into a single globe again. The globes stretched out to form long or short skeins, went into movement again, and were hovering in infinite blue space once more.

Whenever the globes clashed she heard sounds, unbearable sounds, loud enough to make you feel ill. Emma had been dreaming that dream about the noisily clashing globes for years. And now that life was so different, with Hans, and going to town, and Max, it finally dawned on her what sounds they were, and who was making them.

They were screams and the horrible noise of metal being sharpened. And men shouting orders at each other. The words couldn't be made out, only sounds giving orders, commands, making threats, swearing, urging haste.

The scene was a pigsty. Little piglets with no sow, no one to protect them. Squealing in panic, running into the corner, terrified. But the men's hands seized them all the same. Picked them up by the hind legs, one by one, sorted them out. Only the piglets with testicles were for the chop.

There was metal being scoured, knives being whetted and sharpened.

One man pulled each animal's tiny behind apart as if separating the halves of a juicy peach. Another grabbed the piglets' little testicles, which were no bigger than beads. Pulled them out of the piglets' bodies and cut them off. The first man threw the animals back into the sty with blood running down their little legs. None of them had been anaesthetized. None of their wounds was tended; many of them died of the infection that could follow.

The noises that had tormented Emma in her dreams for so many years were a mixture of piglets' squeals, the whetting of knives and the men's loud voices. An infernal cocktail of sound.

She remembered, at last: remembered how she herself had crouched in the corner of the sty where the piglets were bleeding. Her ears had heard it all, her eyes had seen it all. She went unnoticed by the men whom she finally recognised: her father and her grandfather.

After their torture, the piglets were thrown back into the straw, where she was cowering. Now castrated, they bled and squealed miserably.

When Emma woke up she was shaking in horror like a dog in the rain at this memory. She had been spared because she had no balls. Was that what Emma had felt was lucky back then? Lucky that she hadn't been born a boy? Yes, lucky!

For ages, she had secretly feared that she too had been thrown back into the straw. Perhaps she'd been mistaken for a piglet? She'd been lying in the sty with them although she wasn't allowed to be there. Was it possible that her father had

had a son and had cut off his little balls by mistake, and she was all that was left? That she went on living and was called Emma?

Now she was awake and could interpret her dream. All these years, the idea had tormented her: was she a woman or just a castrated boy?

But in that dream, the dream she could interpret at last, there was more than just fear and horror. Emma saw herself lying in the straw with her eyes closed. The squealing piglets in her arms, on her breast. Their bristles thin and soft, their skin like marzipan, their little snouts soft as butter, their eyes moist and their tiny ears trembling with pain and fear.

It would never, ever, have occurred to Emma to castrate her male piglets. She slaughtered them before they were sexually mature, or she exported their meat to Holland, where you could sell pork from boars. It was leaner but had a stronger flavour. Emma never made blood sausage either. When she was alone on the farm at last, she never dipped her hand in the warm blood again. She let it seep into the ground as the Beard-Man had taught her to do.

Next morning the sun was shining. After that strange night, with its dreams and their interpretation, the warm, fragrant earth suddenly seemed to be Emma's sister, like the cow and the butter and the meadow. She was surrounded by nouns of the feminine gender. Like the sun itself in German.

'Hello, Sun, old girl. Going to be hot again today, is it?' And Emma laughed.

Max was sitting on the veranda carving a piece of wood.

She would venture to approach him today.

'Lovely day, isn't it?' asked Emma.

He did not reply.

'That looks nice,' she went on. 'What's it going to be?'

'Nothing,' replied Max.

What was the matter now? No sooner were you reconciled to the world than men started grousing. Went about muttering to themselves, no woman could ever understand why. Then, unexpectedly, Max made a suggestion that surprised Emma very much, coming at this moment.

'Would you mind if we heated the sauna? I'd like to have a sauna again. Of my own free will this time.'

Emma was relieved. So he was talking again.

'Yes, of course, you're welcome.' She hesitated. 'Listen, are you feeling all right?'

'There's nothing wrong with me.'

'A sauna isn't a good idea if you're sick.'

'I'm not sick.'

'I'll heat it up, then. I'd like to do that.'

And Max said, without looking at her, 'Then I'll take my blankets out on the veranda. It would be nice to lie there and rest after the sauna. In the fresh air.'

Emma had already gone a little way off to fetch wood and kindling when he called her back. 'You'll come in the sauna too, won't you?'

She felt nervous. What, the two of them together?

She turned to him. He looked at her and asked, 'What's wrong with that?'

'Mm,' said Emma uncertainly. 'Yes, nothing wrong with it!'

The sauna heated up quickly to a good ninety degrees. Emma had wrapped a huge linen sheet around herself, but what was Max thinking of? Sitting there on the bottom step on his towel, naked. Looking so beautiful, and thinner than on his first night here. Shamelessly showing everything. He hadn't been like that before. Emma rolled her eyes. The man was suddenly so different, talking and talking. She didn't listen very attentively to what he was saying. Something about cars and Wankel engines. As he talked, he put his hand on her knee as if by chance and left it there for a whole sentence. Emma was perspiring both outside and inside.

Soon the sauna was too hot for him, and he wanted to cool off. She would have gone on sitting there, giving him time to take a dip in the stream on his own. But Max simply took her by the hand.

'Come on, Emma. Come in the stream with me.'

She pulled the sheet firmly round her body. Dear God, what was she going to do now? She'd never felt ashamed of herself like that before. Was this something to do with last night too? Or was it because of him and the way he was acting all of a sudden?

Max noticed her reluctance.

"Oh, come on, not ashamed of yourself, are you, Emma?'

'What, me? No, why?'

'You don't have to feel embarrassed.'

He drew her after him. Went over to the slippery little bank of the stream. Cooled his arms, his legs, and then jumped in. She was still standing there wrapped in the sheet.

'Come on in.'

Did he want to see if she was a woman?

There was nothing Emma could do but drop the sheet on the grass. She was afraid of not being beautiful enough. Quickly, she jumped into the water, stood up to her neck in it and felt safer again.

Max came slowly towards her. Smiled at her. Stopped in front of her, took her hand and kissed her, properly this time. She felt his soft lips on her skin. She was a woman, a real woman. Everything about her was all right, and there was a naked man standing here kissing her.

The water was cold, but neither of them seemed to feel it. He had an enchanting smile on his face as he said, untruthfully, 'If I had money I'd go away with you. I'd go to the ends of the earth.'

Her breasts stood out in the cold water. He looked down at them and touched them. Placed his hand on her right breast and held it securely. He didn't have to do any more. He had Emma just where he wanted her.

'I have money,' she confessed obediently.

'Yes?' he said, acting the hypocrite.

'Mm, I have . . . I must tell you . . .'

He put his finger on her lips.

'That doesn't matter now. Tell me afterwards, right?'

Emma nodded. She had fallen into his hands. She was already soft in them, with his arms around her. Her breasts were trembling. He stroked them, kissed her tenderly on the cheek.

They came out of the water, dried themselves on the linen sheets and lay down on the veranda together. Burrowed into the blankets where Max had been sleeping.

Right, Max thought, that's enough. What was that about the money? You were trying to be particularly crafty, weren't you? But it doesn't really bother you, does it?

Emma turned to him, her curving breasts towards him. Rounded, everything rounded. Her shoulders, her hips, her breasts. Under the same blanket with him. Now the image came again, the picture of that silly pressure-cooker he'd seen during the accident. Boiling under great pressure, the valve hissing . . . careful, it's hot.

He felt her belly, so soft. Emma laid her legs on his, wound them around him. He was shaking feverishly, he had a hot, red fit of the shivers. All those *what if* questions melted to nothing at such a temperature. How strong she was. And how beautiful. And how much trust there was in her eyes. She carefully took the cooker off the stove. The pressure was gone, everything was all right. Max was kissing her at last! At this moment his pain discreetly withdrew.

Emma moaned. Her dreams became real flesh, real tongues, saliva sweet as sugar. She licked his mouth like a loving, greedy she-wolf. Max was amazed. He grew, his body became stronger. He could pick her up in his teeth now to kiss her better, kiss her more strongly. She lay in his mouth, trusting him completely, rolling over with happiness.

Within seconds his toenails grew into strong claws. Feathers sprouted on his hands and arms and became wings. His face had grown a beak, dangerously curved, sharp as a knife. His eyes sparkled in the fever of the chase. He seized his prey and swung himself aloft, tried out his huge wingspan. Rose in the air, beating his wings powerfully, circled above the farm and the village rooftops, carrying Emma away with him. Max flew over the tops of the trees to the cold rocks and flung his prey down in his mighty eyrie, where he ripped and tore her apart alive, swallowing piece after piece of her. Emma tasted so wonderful, she was so easy to digest. She flowed out of his pores and created him anew, made him gentle again. Under her tender hands and kisses the eagle lay on his back and turned his vulnerable side to her. His curved beak shrank; he forgot himself entirely.

She looked down at him, stronger than he was, and took him into her. Her belly felt warm and full as if she were eating hot waffles just off the waffle iron, with fresh whipped cream on them. A hundred chocolate marshmallows were nothing to it; her rich mish-mash was low-fat diet food in comparison.

'About the money . . .'
'. . . it doesn't matter.'
'I took it.'
'I know, that doesn't matter either.'

It didn't matter to Max in the straw – even the owl didn't startle him any more. It didn't matter to him in the cool slaughterhouse, in the still-lukewarm sauna, it didn't matter to him on the veranda under the starry sky or in Emma's bed.

Emma told Max about the sparrow chicks her grandfather had thrown against the wall. A human being, another human being who wasn't a child of this farm, listened to her and cursed the old man.

'You're not a sparrow, Emma. You're alive and he's dead.'

A human being. Not imagined, not a dream. A real, live human being with skin and bones, hair, sweat, breath, warmth. Emma felt as if she were merging with Max. She had been so lonely, her throat had burned with every word she spoke to the animals or the plants. But now she lay in the straw, and Max held her in his arms. And Emma talked without stopping. She chattered on, relaxed, told him the tale of the two Whoppers who had been working hard in the fields all day and now had to go back to their village on foot. It was an old story that had been told a thousand times in these parts.

Emma had always just listened. Now she was telling it herself.

'One of them was a small, cheerful fat woman, the other was a huge, tall, cheerful fat woman. As they walked along the path through the fields the big woman suggested taking a short cut across the meadow. But the small woman hesitated. Because there was a bull in the meadow, pawing the ground dangerously with his hooves under a big beech tree that stood on a rise.

'"Suppose he comes closer?" she asked anxiously, pointing to the animal.

'"Oh, he won't," said the other woman, and she raised the top of the barbed wire fence and squeezed through it. The smaller woman followed her.

'The bull never took his eyes off the two women. He raised and lowered his right hoof.

'"Oh," said the small woman, "I'm scared, though."

'"No need to feel scared, I'm with you."

'But the small woman wasn't so sure. "Come on," she begged, "come on! Let's go back on the other side of the fence."

'"Don't worry, he won't hurt you."

'But now the bull moved his heavy body, swaying back and forth.

'"Oh no!" cried the small woman, rather too loudly.

'At that the animal moved. First slowly, then faster and faster, the bull galloped across the meadow towards the women. Then even the big Whopper was scared. The smaller Whopper already imagined herself being gored by those sharp horns, and she screamed. She ran as fast as her short, heavy body would carry her, and she cried, "Come on, run! The bull's coming, come on!"

'But the big Whopper replied, "I'm not running just on account of that bull. I'd sooner have a calf than a heart attack."'

Emma and Max fell about laughing at the punchline, and Max teased Emma by calling her a Whopper.

Suddenly Emma turned serious again and raised her head.

'About the money—'

'Emma!'

'Hans knows, but he doesn't need it any more.'

'. . . it doesn't matter.'

Emma laid her head on Max's chest again, burrowed her nose into his armpit, buried her face in it and drew the smell of him deeply into her.

*E*mma and Max enjoyed every minute of it: eating, sleeping, making love, being together saying nothing, talking, looking at the sky, talking, being together saying nothing, making love, sleeping, eating – nothing had ever been more tender, more delicious.

'Hey, Emma, do you like *coq au vin?*'

'Is that naughty?'

'No,' he laughed. 'It's chicken cooked in wine.'

'Oh, something to eat. I like chicken, but I cook it in water. Nobody around here cooks with wine.'

'Like to try it?'

'Oh, yes. I'll get hold of everything. What do you need?'

'Wine and a chicken.'

So for the second time Emma went to town. She took a huge ham and fifty sausages with her. Not the sausages with the dollar cigars inside, but some that were already air-dried enough to sell.

She parked the tractor outside an electrical goods shop and took her wares in. After much discussion and negotiation she finally exchanged them for a second-hand stereo system and three Handel CDs. She demanded some ready cash as well, and bought wine with it.

Back at the farm she set about providing the chicken. Max was sitting among the beds in the garden when he heard sounds of fluttering and a chase. Too late. What had he done?

Emma had already grabbed one of her chickens by its legs and was holding it upside down. She stood at the wooden block with a short hatchet in her right hand, took aim, and hit the chicken hard on the head with the blunt side of the hatchet. The bird was stunned.

The scream Max had been about to utter died away in his throat. He couldn't even move. This wasn't what he had wanted! Emma placed the chicken's neck on the block and cut its head off with a single, practised blow. The head fell to the ground.

Horrified, Max watched as the chicken freed itself. The headless body struggled so hard that Emma let go of the legs. The chicken jumped off the block and hopped towards Max without any sense of direction at all. It seemed to be asking: why did you do this to me? Why *coq au vin*, for heaven's sake?

At last the bird stopped twitching and its headless body fell over in the dust.

Max made for Emma, walking as the rooster usually did, with long, high-stepping strides.

'What are you doing . . .? Who taught you to . . . but this is frightful! I don't want anything to do with it, anything at all, do you hear? I, for one, am innocent!'

Baffled, Emma put her head on one side. 'But you wanted a chicken, didn't you?'

'I didn't want its head to be cut off!'

'Would you rather cook a chicken with its head still on?'

'Oh, for heaven's sake!'

'Do you want to put the chicken in the wine alive, with its feathers and all?'

'No, I want a proper chicken from the supermarket. Or even better, a frozen chicken wrapped in plastic.'

Spattered with the blood of the fowl, hands on her hips, Emma came towards him.

'So how do you think chickens get into the supermarket and the freezer? Suicide?'

'But it doesn't have to be so bloody, so . . .'

By now Max had realised that she was right. This horrible thing had to be done if you wanted to eat delicious *coq au vin* later.

'Emma, I'm just not used to it, you see. All these nice, cute animals, and then . . .' He held the side of his hand to his throat and mimed slitting his windpipe. 'Arrgh, head off, neck off, belly open, guts spilling out. It's horrible.'

'That's the way it goes,' said Emma laconically. 'Every piece of meat once had a face. If you want to eat meat you have to accept death. If you don't, then don't eat it. There's always ratatouille.'

But Max did want *coq au vin*. So he bravely watched what else happened to the chicken. Emma held it by its feet and plunged it into boiling water, the stump of its neck first. That softened the skin and loosened the feathers.

The stink was horrible. Then Emma began plucking the fowl. Max tried too; he wanted to feel for himself how firmly the feathers stuck in the skin. He plucked one or two out with his fingertips and then left it alone. All he felt was disgust.

Now the bird was washed and laid on the table. Emma cut the belly open. Her hand slipped inside the body cavity and took out the innards. The heart was very small, the liver a joke, the gall bladder was green.

'Where's the pancreas?' asked Max.

'You and your pancreas!' laughed Emma. 'It's much too small to find. I've never seen exactly where it is in a chicken.'

There were still eggs inside the bird. Not just one, but quite a few. A really large one lay close to the chicken's rear end, with a transparent skin round it, only the shell missing. Beyond that was an egg with the same thin skin and a yolk but no white. And even further on was one with a little yolk, and beyond that one with a tiny yolk. They were all lying in the hen's body ready to grow. For the first time Max saw how a hen's egg develops.

Now the chicken finally looked like the chickens in the supermarket. Max could start cooking it. His *coq au vin* succeeded *très bien*.

Meanwhile Emma had unpacked the CD player and proudly put on some Handel. Max was delighted.

Later they both sat on a stout branch of the big chestnut tree in the farmyard, dangling their legs. The prickly green nuts already hung heavy among the leaves, waiting for autumn. Which of them would fall off the branch first, Max wondered, him or the chestnuts? He was relieved to hear Emma chattering away without a care in the world.

'When I was a little girl I used to sit up here every day,' she said, 'watching the chickens. They all know their place. They don't settle it among themselves, it depends how often the rooster has it off with which hen. The hen he picks most often gets the best food and first go at the feeding trough and the fresh water.'

Max listened, fascinated. Emma pointed to one of the chickens. 'That hen is the First Lady, top of the pecking order. You can tell her by her magnificent feathers. She eats well, she's proud, so she walks very upright. And you can also tell her by the bald patch on the back of her neck. That's where the rooster pecks hard to keep his balance when he's having it off from behind. He pulls out her neck feathers. The balder that patch on a hen is, the more often he has it off with her. It's only the rooster who gives her status. That makes her lay eggs happily, sometimes two a day. And the most miserable chicken is exactly the other way around: sparse, dull feathers, almost ragged-looking. But she keeps the feathers at the back of her neck. There, do you see that chicken?'

Max saw it.

'A chicken like that is stressed and frustrated and so she hardly lays any eggs. The rooster declares her fit only for chicken soup. He gives the signal for her death, not me.'

From then on Max sat still for hours and days in the tree, watching the chickens. The hen who was top of the pecking order had a proud, gentle, confident way of walking. She ruffled up her feathers and was very much at home in the poultry yard, particularly just after the act.

When she came stalking up the thin hen had to scurry off, make way, give up her own worm. The chickens in between them took sides, mostly for the strong hen. Any chicken standing up for the weak hen was shunted aside, downgraded.

One day the hen who was second in the pecking order ventured to challenge the First Lady. The proud young thing stalked towards the rooster, brazenly offering herself. The rooster didn't even have to go his rounds any more, he took the tart who offered herself to him several times a day. The old First Lady lost her place and suffered. But the rooster just didn't have the staying power to satisfy his old love and the new one at the same time. The other chickens were quick to notice. They began ignoring their queen and finally shooed her away from the food bowl and the water trough. She was even pecked out of the way by her own former courtiers. Within a week the fowl was finished. A few faithful friends fell from grace with her. But the hens who had been in league with the new First Lady rose in the pecking order along with the tart who was now their queen.

Not a single hen laid an egg while this power struggle went on. Only when the pecking order was clear did everyday life resume, and peace reigned in the poultry yard.

Soon, like any good farmer, Max knew which chicken would be the one to use next time he made *coq au vin*.

Emma had long ago realised that humans were very like chickens.

'The baker's fat wife with the bare patch behind her neck is pregnant again,' she laughed, 'while thin, unmarried Emma is just meat for the pot, fit only for soup.'

'Yes, my little chicken,' agreed Max, who approached her

cackling, and bit her lovingly on the back of the neck. 'Shall I have you roasted, then, or make you happy like a nice fat hen?'

'Oh, please, pull some of my feathers out,' squawked the chicken. And he didn't wait to be asked twice. He could do it better and more gently than a rooster.

As they lay quietly side by side later, Max listened. For the first time in his life he heard silence. Nothing but silence. To his surprise, he realised that all his life before there had always been something to hear. The sound of sirens, thunderstorms, pneumatic drills, weeping, an express train, a plane coming in to land, roars of excitement from football crowds. All mixed up together.

He had never before consciously noticed the effort he made to tolerate all these noises, cope with them, put them in order. For the first time he realised how the noise had shocked and shaken him. He had celebrated Christmas forty times, but he'd never really known the silence of the night.

Emma lay in his arms, drenched with sweat and satisfied. The smell of that is like no other. Sweet, heavy. And all was still. He took a deep breath and grinned.

'What is it?' asked Emma.

He looked at her and smiled. 'Happy. Very happy.'

'Ah,' sighed Emma, stroking his face.

He pointed to some little bluish, reddish marks on her skin and asked, 'Did I do that?'

Emma shook her head. 'It's erysipelas. Butchers get it, and chefs and dealers in game. An occupational hazard. It's carried by pigs.'

'Does it hurt?'

'No, just itches and burns a little.'

'Is that bad?'

'No, not bad. Not infectious either, or I think not.'

She hesitated for a moment, and then went on.

'Max?'

'Hm?'

She sat up, took his hand, and asked, 'And what do you have?'

'What would I have?'

'You do have something, don't you? You're not well.'

He shook his head.

'You're so thin. I can feel your bones.'

'Don't worry, I've always been thin.'

'Won't you go and see a doctor?'

Max just shook his head again and said nothing.

But Emma knew. She had learned to recognise every sign of sickness in her animals. They got better quickly or not at all. The pigs infected each other, and she had to watch out for that too. If necessary you could kill a pig before disease took hold. Then at least its meat was fit for sale. She'd been watching Max. He had constipation at some times, diarrhoea at others. His legs were swollen. He suffered from wind. His eyes were yellow. Emma noticed that his liver was hardly functioning, although he drank very little alcohol, so it was something else. Something worse.

When she touched his stomach it hurt him. He didn't eat much. He refused her sausage, he refused butter, anything fatty – he probably couldn't digest it. But he still thought he could pretend to her. She let him think so. She had him here, and she was enjoying every day he spent with her.

Emma had the rare ability to leave other people alone and respect their wishes.

Max lay in Emma's bed. The window was open, and the early autumn sun made the chestnut leaves outside shine. Houseflies played above the bed. That was the first thing he'd seen when he opened his eyes in Emma's house. After the accident. The flies were still playing the same game. In this time, in these few weeks, everything that made his life worth living had happened.

What luck that he'd survived the accident.

'Why do the flies play that game?' he asked Emma.

'I always like to watch them doing it. Maybe just for fun. I don't know.'

'We must play Catch, just the two of us, you and me,' he said, and fell silent. Let it go on, he thought, let it go on for ever and ever, and he knew that it wouldn't.

The rooster didn't talk to her any more. The TV presenter presented the show, that was all. The raven had flown away. The moped had served its purpose.

It was getting difficult to wash the mincer, the sausage-making machine stuck, the wooden trough had a leak in it. The knives were blunt; where on earth was Flachsmeier? In his young days he'd had an Italian girlfriend called Laura. He wanted to marry her. But she fell down a ravine when she was out walking, just fell to her death after breakfast one morning in May.

Emma whetted the knives herself, but without any pleasure

or sense of purpose. Max had been sitting in the pigsty for days, getting to know the animals. He particularly liked the one with the black spots on its back.

Today it was that pig's turn.

'You can't mean it!' wailed Max. 'It's so sweet! How can you slaughter it?'

'How? With a knife, of course!'

He'd been standing by the fence with that one, of all the pigs. The animal had scratched itself against the wood of the fence in ecstasy, its back moving up and down and then up and down again. And the look on its face! It had been rolling its eyes with delight.

'Such a cute pig! It loves life. Choose another one.'

'Fine,' Emma had said. 'I'll choose another one.'

And she chose the one with the drooping ear. But he didn't want her to take that one either, because he'd been down to the stream with it when it went to wallow, which it did in a big way. The animal had lain down by the bank to roll about in the mud. Later, in between two saunas, Max had ventured down to the soft mud himself and smeared and rubbed his calves with it. There were tiny grains of sand in the mud, and they gave his skin a nice massage. At first he went in only up to his knees, but then he actually smeared himself all over with soft, warm mud. And laughed at himself, laughed out loud.

'You old pig, you!' Emma had called.

The pig had let the mud dry on its skin in the sun. After getting filthy like that, Max had washed in the stream. Afterwards they felt like brothers, as well as being clean and refreshed.

'Why the one with the drooping ear? Just because I'm fond of it, right?'

'It's how I earn money,' she said defiantly.

'Do something else to earn money. You could, you could . . .'

'Yes, what? What could I do?'

'You could . . . you could crochet! Make crochet table-cloths, that's what other women do!'

'Crochet, yuk!' cried Emma in revulsion.

She bravely picked up her knife and enticed the pig with the black spots to follow her into the yard and under the block and tackle. The pig happily followed her.

'Don't go, don't go!' Max warned the animal. But it trotted on.

Then he snapped at Emma. 'You're abusing those pigs' trust in you!'

But she stuck to her guns. She had to kill the pigs. He went off into the fields.

However, Emma had to work in order to live, to feed them both. So she did what she usually did. She petted the animal, told it stories. She made a huge effort, but something had changed. She couldn't even raise the knife.

Emma let the pig go. It trotted happily back to the meadow, where it lay down in the wallow.

Max found Emma in the straw. She looked depressed. He took her in his arms and asked her to forgive him.

'You're right,' she said. But she knew she had lost her career.

I call the old sow into the witness box,' ordered the Supreme Judge, making his request official by hitting the table hard, three times, with his wooden mallet. He struck so vigorously that white powder drifted out of the venerable gentleman's musty wig. The hunchbacked court usher opened the heavy doors of the hall, and the old sow, swaying back and forth, her legs spread wide, trotted into court. She turned her little eyes, sunk in their rings of fat, to the whispering spectators. Carnivores gaping at her, every last one of them. She didn't know anyone here.

She dragged herself on. Her fat belly brushed the cracked wooden floor, her teats hung low, empty and useless. One of them was swollen and inflamed. Whenever the sore teat touched the floor the old sow twitched with pain. As she did so the last of the old bristles on her fat body shook.

Now she was level with the defendant, who kept her head lowered. The old sow stopped, turned ponderously aside and tried to meet the defendant's eyes. But she hid her face in both hands, slumping. Tears were running through her fingers.

The old sow gave her an affectionate grunt before she made her way on to the judge, breathing heavily.

'. . . and nothing but the truth?'

'So help me God,' gasped the sow asthmatically.

And she added, 'I ask to be allowed to decline to give evidence.'

'Request refused, my dear madam.' There was something supercilious in the judge's voice. 'Unless,' he added, pausing and grinning nastily, 'unless you can credibly assure me that you are related to the accused either by blood or by marriage.'

How absurd! The spectators roared with laughter. The boom of the judge's mallet warned the carnivores to keep quiet, even though he had egged them on himself. This man, the sow now realised, was not a good judge.

And his mallet was too loud for the poor animal. The public reacted obediently to its banging and fell silent. But the sow couldn't stand the harsh noise. It went through her ear and straight into her brain. A pig can't pretend to be deaf. Every high or harsh sound, every sudden loud noise, every hissing current of air hurts a pig, sends the animal crazy.

The defendant was aware of that. She knew the sow well. Full of sympathy, she finally looked at her. She understood why the old sow's muzzle was twisted in pain.

But the judge didn't understand at all.

'What was your relationship with the accused?'

'We were very close.' Her voice was low, pleading for peace and quiet.

'What do you mean, close?'

'We meant a lot to each other.'

'What do you mean by that?'

'We used to squeeze each other nice and hard.'

'Squeeze each other with what?'

The sow looked hard at the judge. Why couldn't the man up there understand?

'With our backs, with our sides, with our bellies, all depending on how we lay.'

Yet again the spectators roared. Yet again the wooden mallet banged noise into the pig's brain.

Enemies! thought the sow. Her worst enemies were here, banging mallets and roaring. This scum ought to be in the dock themselves.

From then on the old sow stopped grunting and answered no more questions. She simply refused to give evidence.

The judge threatened her with detention in custody for contempt of court if she wouldn't give a full and reasonable account.

But the sow remained obstinate. Then the judge told the ushers to take her away. The men tied a dirty rope around the fat sow's neck, choking her, pulled her, tried to get her out of the courtroom and into the cells.

The sow braced her front trotters like a stubborn donkey. She squealed with fear. The men pulled. They were strong as horses. The defendant couldn't bear it any more.

She clicked her tongue, a soft, familiar sound. No one else could hear it in all the uproar, only the sow. She glanced at the defendant, and the defendant nodded to her. At that the sow called, with the last of her strength, 'I'll talk, I'll talk.'

The judge ordered the sow to be brought forward again, but the rope must stay tied around her neck. One of the ushers stood beside her, holding her where she was.

And the old sow gave evidence.

'I had eight piglets at the time, not a stillbirth among them, all of them good sound piglets, doing well. A week after I had them the ninth fell into my sty. From the hatch up in the roof above, where the straw usually comes down, it just fell in! It was cold, it was crying. I thought to myself, oh, this is too much! I'll bite it, I'll kick it to death, what's this strange piglet doing here? But then I felt sorry for it. It held me tight. I lay down and thought: well, fancy that. Then it lay down too. With my other eight piglets. It squeezed up against me, nice and hard and firmly. It warmed itself on me.'

The judge said nothing, the spectators said nothing, and finally the mallet fell silent too.

'Otherwise it would have died, it was so cold. Later it got close to my teats, it drank greedily, it was even hungrier than the others!'

At this point the sow smiled. The memory of suckling the piglet made her beam like any other proud mother.

'And it stayed there. Always on the same teat. It's the one that . . .'

The sow stopped. She had been going to say: the one that still oozes pus. The one that hurts me so much.

But a mother gives everything. A mother doesn't complain, she suffers in silence. So the old sow stopped in the middle of her sentence and swallowed the rest of it.

'It was different from the others. It went away in the night and came back next day. The other eight grew fat, but not the ninth. It sucked more than they did, but it never grew fat. I still thought it would die some time. But it stayed alive. The others

186

were taken away. Time and again I suffered torments of grief. Then the one that stayed comforted me. I had more piglets, it suckled with them. Later it ate out of the trough like me. It didn't grow much, it never got fat. It was never taken away, only the others.'

The judge didn't understand. He frowned and asked, 'What, pray, does the piglet that stayed with you have to do with the defendant?'

The fat sow put her head on one side, looked guilelessly at the judge, and said, 'What do you mean? Don't you understand? She *is* the ninth piglet!'

The spectators still didn't get it. There was whispering in the back rows. 'What's the sow saying? What did she say?'

The judge leaned forward, looked the sow sternly in the eye. 'The accused is not a pig. She is a human being.'

'Oh, come on!' said the sow indignantly. 'She may look like one, but she was mine. I suckled her, fed her, comforted her, loved her and brought her up.'

'Like a piglet?'

'Instead of a child, yes.'

The judge's voice was sarcastic. 'So you don't bear your ninth piglet any grudge?'

'Me? Why me of all pigs? No.'

'She stands accused of murder.'

'That's silly! Who's she supposed to have murdered?'

'She murdered the piglets you bore. She's accused of having killed them with her own hands – and intentionally, note that.'

The sow shook her head.

'She is even accused of eating the bodies!'

The spectators were shaking with delight to hear such a scandalous story. But the judge hadn't finished yet.

'She cut the throats of your entire family. And you stay calm?'

The sow explained, 'But only to end our lives with warmth. She did it full of love. She wasn't murdering them when she wielded the knife so confidently, she was ending their lives.'

Now the judge levelled the forefinger of his right hand at the sow like a spear. 'So she *did* cut their throats?'

'Well, yes.'

'With a knife?'

'Very gently, with a very sharp knife, without any pain.'

'Guilty!' cried the judge. 'She stuck those pigs. The witness statement is concluded.'

And the mallet came down on the table again with a loud bang.

'Guilty as accused.'

Confused, the old sow tried to meet the defendant's eyes. The rope kept her from turning.

'In the name of the people, I pass the following sentence . . .'

The spectators were roaring. 'Throw her to the pigs for them to eat!'

'Do as you would be done by!'

'An eye for an eye, a tooth for a tooth!'

The judge banged his wooden mallet on the table again, on and on without stopping. Then the old sow ran wild. She screamed, broke free, smashed tables and benches, splintered wood. Injured people were bleeding. The ushers ran to restrain the frantic sow. They tied her up and dragged her away. The sow was squealing with fear.

*E*mma woke drenched with sweat. It was as if she had opened a door into another room. As if she had finally remembered something forgotten, something that had always been on the tip of her tongue and yet never passed her lips.

It was so monstrous, at first light of dawn it set off such mingled horror and happiness in her, that she was glad not to be alone at this moment. She was glad he was lying beside her. She moved close to Max, who was still asleep. Snuggled up to his back, passed her hands over his chest. They had little bristles too, masculine bristles. Safe like that, Emma could let the images of her dream pass before her mind's eye again.

Max woke up.

'What is it? Can't you sleep?' he asked.

'I had a dream.'

'A bad dream?'

'No. Well, I don't know yet.'

'Tell me. I'm listening.'

'As a child I once fell into the pigsty. I was still very small, only a toddler. Like you the other day, I fell down the hatch from the straw loft into the sow's sty. She'd just had her litter. They're dangerous then, just about exhausted after giving birth to eight piglets or so. They're unpredictable.'

'That's what you dreamed?'

'Yes, I mean no, it really happened. I remember it. I fell through the hatch. But the bit I'd forgotten was that no one wondered where I was. No one came looking for me.'

Emma shook her head, because now she remembered it all clearly. She had even lain down at the sow's side with the other piglets.

She looked at him, horrified.

'I sucked milk from her teats! Isn't that dreadful?'

Max didn't think it was any big deal. 'Other people drink mare's milk. They eat frog's legs or slimy snails or swallow live oysters.'

Emma stroked her cheeks and forehead with her fingers. The huge sow's head was right above her face. She licked Emma's face with her firm, rough tongue. That's what had happened, and it had been wonderful.

It hadn't been like that just once, the time when she fell into the pigsty crying, it went on for a long, long time. Whenever she shed tears the sow licked them away.

Emma lay close to Max's back and remembered. She'd had no other comfort. It meant so much and yet so little. When she had to take refuge, when she needed to cry, she had gone into the pigsty with the sow.

Emma had cried because she'd been beaten. Hit in the face and on the head with a wooden spoon and a clothes hanger, beaten on her shoulders and back and her bare little toddler's bottom. So hard that the wooden spoon and clothes hanger broke. Until her skin was burning red.

She had cried when they made her look ridiculous.

When she was scalded.

Left out in the cold.

Burned.

Wedged fast somewhere. Pinched.

Woken from sleep.

Molested on the loo.

When her hair was pulled.

When leather boots kicked her.

When her face was pushed down in the dirt.

When her arm was twisted until it broke.

When Emma wet her bed, night after night. She was left lying in it. It stank worse than the pigsty.

When she was locked in she had banged the back of her head against the door. Again and again and again. But no one would hear her, no one let her out.

It all went black before Emma's eyes. The memory made her feel sick.

'I hid,' she went on, her voice faltering, 'I hid from the beatings and the anger for days on end. As far as they were concerned I'd disappeared, I could have died of hunger and thirst. No one bothered about me, no one missed me, no one came looking for me.'

Emma stared ahead of her for a long time. Her true mother had been an old sow, her siblings squealing piglets, some of them castrated. At least she'd had a family. A kind of family.

After a long silence, Max asked, 'What about your mother?'

'My mother? That meant threatening footsteps coming my way.'

'And your father?'

'My father meant cowardly footsteps going away from me.'

Max took her in his arms. 'Oh, my girl, my dear girl.'

With him her pulse beat rhythmically again, her breath came evenly. She clung to his thin body. It was her prop and stay. At last she could let her anger out. She was trembling with old fears; he caressed them away. She cried out, and Max held her tight.

That evening Emma lit a bonfire on the place where the Ferrari had burned. She threw everything that had belonged to her grandfather on the flames: his uniforms, his Nazi Party membership book, his decorations and his black leather boots, all of it. And the coat hangers, the wooden spoons, the leather strap, the pitchfork. Into the fire with them all. She had no idea why she'd kept those things so long.

'You ought to forgive them,' said Max.

'No,' said Emma. 'No. I'm not forgiving them. My anger does me good. It's not turning in on me and hurting any more. It's freeing itself and dripping out of me. I'll let it run for years. When that flow of pus dries up, then I'll forgive. Not before.'

Everything that wouldn't burn but had to be out of her sight had to be taken away from the farm. Emma put it on the farm cart. The one with the hydraulic lift so that you could tip it backwards. All of a sudden it was easy to get rid of all that horrible stuff and throw it away. She coupled the tractor to the loaded cart.

As she drove through the village with a century's worth of rubbish, the Whoppers wondered what on earth was going on at the pig farm.

'See that Emma, driving about in her petticoat? She forgot to put on her overall!'

'Must have gone crazy.'

'It'll be on account of the auction.'

'That don't mean there's a reason to go driving about stark naked.'

'What'll she do now, without the farm?'

'They say as how there's a fellow just widowed in What's-its-name, over beyond Hegeholz. With five kids.'

'Ooh, but he drinks.'

'Better than nowt, though.'

'Why don't she take Henner, then?'

'Henner, he'll get the living daylights beat out of him if he takes her!'

Emma couldn't have cared less about the Whoppers and their gossip. She drove to the local tip, started the hydraulic device and buried her rubbish.

*M*ax was in such pain that he almost lost consciousness. It knocked him off his feet. He lay on the kitchen floor, bent double. His entire back was burning. He howled and wept with the sorrow of parting. Wept miserably. Before she came back he managed to drag himself to Emma's bed. She found him in it, fast asleep.

Over the next few days he just wanted to lie there listening to Handel. Music had been a comfort to his parents; they used to put records on and go to concerts together when words were out of place, and the pain of life was getting too much for them.

Minuets by Mozart had cheered them, stern fugues by Bach restored order to their lives, when they listened to Telemann trumpet concertos his parents believed in God again, and Handel gave them a sense of being something special. His parents seldom listened to music by Tchaikovsky or Beethoven, because those composers seemed to them too perfect.

A few days later, one late summer's day, Max wanted to share this legacy with Emma. He put the loudspeakers of the stereo in the window facing the farmyard. He put on Handel's Water Music, found the place he liked so much: the place where it sounds as if the king himself were walking in with great dignity.

He cleared a path right through the farmyard, putting the buckets, troughs and implements aside. Swept the yard with the old besom broom, found a large wicker basket and picked all the flowers he could find in the garden and the fields. Every last one of them. Then he scattered flowers over the yard. When Emma came back from a walk she was amazed.

What was the idea of all this?

Then Max took all the sleeveless overalls out of Emma's bedroom, Emma's own, her mother's and her grandmother's. He had found a leftover belt that had belonged to her father.

'What are you doing?'

'Come here, come here!' he called to her.

Max strung all the overalls together, putting the belt through straps on both sides. Strung together like that and pulled tight around Emma's waist, the overalls made a huge and colourful skirt. As wide as if it had a crinoline underneath. So long that it brushed elegantly over the ground.

She felt as if she were on stage, or in a carnival procession.

Finally he put a garland of flowers on the startled Emma's hair. She was still laughing at his funny idea when the music began to play. It was loud, very loud, as it rang out over the farmyard. Max stepped back.

There stood Emma in a huge skirt, her hair crowned with flowers. And a path of flowers in front of her. He signalled to her to walk along it. Emma carefully stepped on to the carpet of flowers, moving in time to Handel's Water Music.

The animals came and lined the path; they all wanted to see her, to take a look at the dress. The chickens, the rooster, the pigs, the cow, the dog. Emma was moved. She felt a sense of solemnity: she wasn't just walking any more but promenading with dignity past her little court. She felt lighter, she felt warmer, she proudly raised her chin, her shoulders relaxed and dropped. Her body lost its tension, her breasts were turned to the sun. Emma drew fresh air into her lungs, her heart was beating in time, Emma's skin was taut.

By the time she reached the end of the path her legs felt very light. She turned around and around, first slowly, then faster and faster. The skirt fluttered in the wind when the trumpets played. The brightly coloured overalls opened out like the petals of flowers, and Emma was dancing in the middle of it all, her arms spread wide, going round and round until the music died away.

Little as Max had known about the land before, about dirt and blood and tears, Emma had known just as little about music and dancing. Her world of pigs had been limited; now it opened wide. Emma moved with wild abandon, but inside she felt calmer, more relaxed, more secure. Their wonderful conversations about anything and everything had brought a smile to her face as if by magic, and it made Max feel good. It gave him the feeling that he hadn't lived in vain.

He felt even more triumphant when, a day after dancing to Handel, Emma ventured to make another foray into life, this time one of a very feminine kind: she realised she had nothing to wear.

Emma drove to town, went into the best and biggest

197

department store there, and found a young, red-headed sales-girl. She put the last of her money into the girl's hand and said, 'Could you please help me to choose some clothes?'

The two of them worked their way through the entire ladies' outerwear and underwear departments. Emma tried on everything the salesgirl brought her. Chose this, decided against that. Her liking for strong colours hadn't changed, but the clothes were no longer cut like overalls. Soon she was kitted out. The girl got her grandmother's linen petticoat as a present, and thanked Emma with a happy, 'Wow, terrific!'

Hans too noticed Emma's new clothes when he arrived at the farm. Max was asleep and didn't hear the car.

Hans and Emma greeted each other like old friends.

'It's going to work. We've given Happy Pork a good start. I tell you, this is going to be a hit. A real hit.'

'I don't know what you're talking about.'

'We're offering pig breeders a franchise . . . we'll find colleagues of yours who'll agree to rear and slaughter pigs by your method. We guarantee that their animals will be treated as well as yours, live happy lives and then die happy. The meat of pigs like that is top quality: it's firmer and redder, and it has a particularly good flavour. Completely pure and uncontaminated, so it can be sold for three times the price of ordinary pork. I've registered a trademark and patented the method.'

'But what's that got to do with me?'

'You?' Hans grinned. 'You'll be able to live on it.'

Emma didn't believe him. Hans gave her an advance. Emma

took the money, but she still didn't believe him. She would give him those dollars back. She was just going to tell him about the sausages when Hans asked about Max. Emma took him into the bedroom and left the two of them alone. When Hans came back to the kitchen an hour later the muscles of his face were working, but he shed no tears.

'Help him,' was all he said.

Hans went out, and Emma saw him hitting the roof of the car with his fist and then leaning on the vehicle for a moment with his face hidden. Finally he got in and drove away.

That evening Emma and Max sat on the veranda, wrapped in blankets. The evenings were cooler now.

'Have you ever been to Mexico?' Max asked.

'I've been to town at last. Nowhere else.'

Then Max told her about Mexico, about the Mexicans, his island there, the beach, the Mayan hut.

'Why don't we go there together?' Max suggested. And he described the way the pelicans caught fish in the Gulf of Mexico. Emma saw that it did him good to talk about Mexico. So she humoured him by making travel plans with him, but she knew they would never go anywhere together now.

*T*he village farmers had already brought in their harvest. It hadn't escaped Henner's notice that Emma's roots were still in the ground and her meadows had not been mown. The moped had been quiet for a long time, and the village children brought no more sausages back from Emma's farm.

He drove up to see her, feeling both worried and curious. When he entered the house, he had a surprise. The place was clean and tidy. And Emma was completely different. She was very quiet.

'What's the matter with you?'

'I'm clearing up, Henner. I mean, I have to leave the farm. Or did I win the lottery after all?'

'No, I'm afraid not.'

'Well, then you see I have to clear up first.'

'You, clear up? Since when did you ever clear anything up? This is all quite new!'

'Everything's all right, Henner.'

She put her arms around him and gave him a hug. Henner was totally confused. Emma had never done a thing like that before.

She didn't want to see anyone any more, not the baker's wife and certainly not Henner's mother. So she did all her shopping in the next village.

Up in the attic she had found an old brown suitcase held together by a strap. She cleaned it up and carefully polished the leather with furniture cream until it looked reasonably all right again. She packed everything she was going to take with her in this case. Meanwhile Max lay down below in her bed, his face distorted by pain, looking out of the window.

She asked him, to distract his mind, 'Did you ever have a pet at home?'

'No, never,' he said, grateful for a change of ideas. 'My mother was afraid I'd get used to it, I'd love it, and then if it happened to . . .' He stopped short.

To die, Emma finished the sentence in her thoughts. We can't talk about it – why doesn't he say 'die'?

'No, wait a moment!' Max had thought of something. 'I did once have a pet.'

She stayed behind the wardrobe door where he wouldn't see her tears.

'I had a tapeworm! It came out of me. I gave birth to it on the loo. I was five at the time. It took the tapeworm forever to come out – must have been fifteen minutes.'

Now she couldn't help laughing. 'You gave birth to a tapeworm?'

'It was incredibly long, a metre long.'

'Yuk!' she said, laughing. His disgust threshold had sunk dramatically since he had come to her farm.

She made Max some good, strong soup and fed it to him,

because all his strength was gone. Then she wrapped him in warm blankets and carried him to his favourite place on the veranda. It was late afternoon. Insects were buzzing in the warm air; a few plants in the garden had new flowers on them.

Emma stood with her back to Max, held tight to the railings, and looked out at the garden.

'What is it?'

'Cancer.'

'How do you know?'

'I saw a doctor.'

'Can anything be done?'

'No.'

'How much longer?'

'Any time now.'

'Are you in pain?'

'Yes, bad pain.'

'What can I do for you?'

Now she turned and held his gaze.

'You must help me, Emma. You must help me.'

Only in front of the registrar did Emma and Max find out each other's surnames.

The formally clad gentleman read out of a black book. 'And as your married surname you choose Wachs?'

'Yes,' said Emma, whose surname was Wachs.

Max interrupted. 'Hang on. Wachs? You mean my name will be Wachs, as in "wax"?'

Emma shrugged her shoulders. 'What about it? Men can take their wives' names just as well as the other way around.'

'But then I'll be called Max Wachs. It rhymes. It sounds like . . . Max Wachs, it sounds like a dog barking.'

'Yes, I see,' Emma agreed, and tried another solution. 'Then let's have a double-barrelled surname.'

The registrar looked at his papers and tried to suppress a smile. He didn't succeed. He started laughing and laughed until tears were running down his face. After a while he pulled himself together and said, 'Bienen-Wachs, then . . . "Beeswax"!'

Which set him off again, and he began spluttering with laughter behind his solemn-looking desk.

Emma was at a loss. 'Your surname is Bienen, as in "bees"?'

'I'll enter Bienen as the married surname. Neither husband nor wife chooses to take a double-barrelled name. Herr and Frau Bienen, allow me to congratulate you.'

In short order, Emma Bienen took out the first passport she'd held in her life, and Max booked a one-way flight to Cancun in Mexico.

His body was so thin, he was just skin and bone. Emma carried him over the threshold of her house. Another wave of pain took hold of him and refused to end. He lay in her arms shaking, rolled his yellow eyes, and threw up on her wedding dress.

'Sorry.'

'In future you throw up without saying sorry, agreed?'

The pain was taking despotic command of every part of his body. Max couldn't move his arm any more. It just twitched.

His eyes saw nothing now, his guts were galloping in time to the whiplashes of pain. Now and then Max had lucid moments and was briefly the same as before. Then Emma joked with him, saying 'Beeswax,' and Max laughed.

He stroked her breasts and she stroked his prick, which would have liked another little game, but it stayed limp as the prick of an old man who feels more comfortable in his armchair.

The pain came back, torturing Max as never before. It was burning him alive. He said no more, hoped for nothing, wanted nothing, wasn't really alive. But he screamed with pain worse than ever. His eyes begged for help.

What am I to do? Emma asked herself, but she had known the answer for a long time.

Emma carried Max out into the farmyard and sat down under her block and tackle. She laid his body on the basalt paving and took his head in her lap. She stroked his hair and his sides again and again. Stroked him, caressed him gently, talked to him. Max didn't hear her words. He was gasping for air like a fish pulled out of the water on to dry land. His eyelids fluttered. With a huge effort he opened them and stared at Emma.

She held him tightly around the shoulders with her right arm. Couldn't do it. Laid him down again.

She couldn't do it – no one could do it. Emma slumped forward and shed tears into his shirt.

Max was twitching and breathing stertorously. With one

hand, he groped for her and found her knee. Stroked it. Held it tight. Dug his nails into it.

Then, suddenly, the rooster came along. He had been standing at the side of the farmyard. Now, as if shooed away from where he stood by an invisible hand, he came running up as fast as he could. As he ran he beat his clipped wings so strongly that he actually took off from the ground and flew in a circle all around the chestnut tree before landing again in a fright.

See? You can do anything if you try!

Then Emma took her long, sharp knife and at last, unhesitatingly, she swiftly cut Max's throat with a single, precise movement. He cried out briefly and then lay still. Emma was shaking with fear and horror. His blood spurted from the wound. She held him tight. Dissolving in tears, she counted, 'One, two, three, four, five, six, seven, eight.'

Emma had been so afraid it wouldn't be the same for him as for the pigs. So very afraid! But now he lay still in her arms with his blood running out on the stone, seeping away between the paving stones.

Max had closed his eyes. Emma sobbed with grief. Trembling, feeling wretched, she said, 'Thank you for keeping me company, I've loved you so much, so much. It doesn't hurt, you see. I promised you it wouldn't hurt. Goodbye, dear Max. Goodbye, my Max, dear Max.'

It was the greatest effort Emma had ever made. No pig had been heavier, no grandfather more terrible. It was hard to have deprived yourself of the best thing you had. Yet Emma knew it was the right thing to do. No one ought to die worse than a pig.

Emma put the bloodstained knife aside. She would never pick up a knife again, never.

She carried Max's body up to her bed, placed his hands over his chest and lovingly covered him up.

She washed, threw her bloodstained clothes away, changed and took the leather suitcase that she had packed and left ready. She put it on the passenger seat of her tractor.

Then she went to the farm buildings, opened all the doors and fences, every gate, every trapdoor, gave the cow a last pat, kissed the old sow, the strong boar, all the pigs. Last of all she said goodbye to her rooster.

He didn't make a sound. All the animals were quiet, even the fowls. And the wind.

Emma got on the tractor and drove away from the farm. In the dirt beside the accelerator she found one last little chocolate marshmallow. She picked it up and threw it behind her. That brought her animals back to life. The chickens fell on it, all except the rooster. He crowed and crowed after her. So that was that.

*S*oon afterwards a message came through to Henner: a tractor registered in his police district, licence plate H0G-CK 58, had been left outside the airport's main entrance. He replied that there was something wrong here – he knew the owner, he was sure she'd never drive her old tractor to the airport, yes, he was one hundred per cent certain.

At that moment his old mother rushed into the police station, loudly and venomously complaining that Emma's filthy boar had been churning up her lovely front garden – it was a total wreck! And Emma's rooster had been having it off with the baker's wife's favourite hen.

Once again Henner was unable to prevent his mother from filling the police car with smoke. When they drove into Emma's farmyard he told her, in a threatening tone, 'You stay sitting at the back there! This is my work, get it?'

She grunted in surprise and rolled herself another cigarette while the old one was still in the corner of her mouth.

Henner found a scene of disaster in the bedroom. So Emma had carried out her threat. Someone had come along to look round her farm with the auction sale in mind. And he'd come to the sticky end predicted by Emma herself. *If anyone tries taking my farm away I'll stick him like a pig.*

She had cut his throat. She had actually gone and slaughtered him. Henner was badly shaken. He went downstairs to the kitchen and sat down to get control of himself and think what to do.

Finally he went back to his car, and using his radio asked Karl to come up here, and please not to use the siren.

His mother pricked up her ears: something had happened. She sat perfectly still and didn't move a muscle. In his agitation Henner had almost forgotten she was there.

A little later Karl drove into the farmyard, and the two men went indoors. With difficulty, the old woman squeezed her way out of the car. She found the bloody patch under the block and tackle. Saw the bloodstained knife, picked it up and examined it for a long time.

Upstairs, Karl was standing by the bed.

'Oh, my word!' the fire chief commented on seeing the corpse. 'He's dead.'

'Well spotted, Karl. And what are we going to do with him?'

'Has Emma gone?'

Henner nodded.

'So who's this?'

Henner shrugged.

Karl shook his head. 'You never know anything.' And he added, 'Know what I think?'

'Nope, what do you think?'

'Your Emma's made off. And she killed this guy first.'

'That's what I think too. I reckon he wanted the farm, and she stuck him. She'd even told me she would.'

Karl looked at Henner in alarm. 'She told you in advance?'

'Yup.'

'So what did you . . .?'

'I thought . . . I mean I knew she *could* do it. But to think she really did . . .'

Karl shook his head again. He bent over the body and examined it. As fire chief he had learnt a lot about the human body and resuscitation techniques, and he had seen a good many corpses. They lay on the motorway or the highway, wedged into their cars. Corpses held no terrors for Karl any more. He took a closer look at the body with its throat slit.

'Very thin, just skin and bone. Jaundiced, bloated stomach. This man was sick. Mortally sick.'

They found Max's papers in the pocket of his trousers.

'Max Bienen.'

Henner's mother had stolen quietly into the house. She had stopped on the bottom step of the wooden staircase and was listening. She still had the knife in her hand.

'Then ask your head office to find out who he is and if anyone's looking for him. And then get them searching for Emma.'

'Nope, I reckon I won't do that,' said Henner. 'I'm not having them go after Emma and charging her and putting her on trial. For murder or something horrible like that, she'll be jailed for life. Not our Emma – she'd die in jail.'

'Lots do.'

'But I don't want that, not for Emma. Him there,' said

Henner, pointing to Max, 'you say he was sick. I reckon she helped him, she . . . she . . .'

'Put him out of his misery?'

'That's about it. She put him out of his misery.'

Henner sniffed the air. Nicotine? Sure enough, there was his mother in the doorway, discharging venom in her well-tarred voice.

'Stuck someone like a pig, did she, the slut? Yes? Be going to prison, right? Ha, ha, ha, oh, what a thing, ha, ha, ha!'

Henner took three steps towards her, grabbed the hand in which she was holding the knife, and said in a sharp voice, 'This here, Mother, this is the murder weapon. And the only finger-prints I can make out on it will be yours.'

She stared at her son. How dared he? But he went on holding her hand firmly, and called over to Karl, 'Hey, this in her hand is the murder weapon, right?'

'Right,' agreed Karl. 'Guilty as sin, no doubt about it.'

'Are you two out of your minds?' cried Henner's mother.

But Henner was having no more of this. 'Another squeak out of you, one word in the wrong place, and I'll see *you* in jail. Get it?'

That shut her up.

'And now clear out.'

She cleared out.

Karl nodded respectfully.

The suddenly courageous Henner decided, 'We can't have them looking for Emma.'

'What are you going to do, then? It's our duty.'

Henner defended Emma as only a good friend can. 'Back

then with the Beard-Man you did your duty. But it still weren't right. Now do it the other way around. Do what's not your duty, but what's right.'

Karl took a deep breath and nodded. 'What's against the law is right. So what do we do?'

'This man lying here, he died. He's dead. We'll leave it at that. No one has to know that he just happens to have had all his blood drained away.'

Karl shook his head. And said no more.

Henner informed police headquarters in town that a man by the name of Max Bienen had been found lying dead in bed.

Anything to suggest foul play, any indication that another person was involved?

'No,' said Henner.

Did the body show any outward signs of injury?

'None,' Karl confirmed. And since the two of them were considered so trustworthy, police headquarters decided against visiting the scene of the death and saw no need for a post-mortem. Henner could get a blank death certificate from the local doctor, no problem. He'd picked up the local doctor drunk at the wheel umpteen times and let him off. Well, what use was a country doctor without a driving licence? Exactly.

'And suppose they open up the coffin?'

'Suppose who opens up the coffin?'

'Anyone.'

'We'll put a roll-neck pullover on him,' decided Henner.

Max was placed in a coffin and taken to the town, where he lived. Hans, who had got him a grave beside his parents, made the funeral arrangements.

Henner found a note from Emma saying that the fresh sausages in the drying chamber belonged to the Hilfinger Garage in town. But Henner thought they weren't mature yet. He chose some well-dried sausages instead, and gave Hans those.

Henner and Karl remained the best of friends. Henner's mother wasn't allowed to smoke any more except in the front garden. And Karl no longer felt guilty about the Beard-Man.

At Christmas Karl and his Volunteer Fire Brigade organised a delivery of aid donations to Belarus, as they did every year. Emma's overalls and old underwear and the last of her sausages and hams were part of the consignment. That was what Henner and Karl had decided. And so it was that many Belarusian families, slicing their German sausage, found a rolled-up wad of dollar bills falling out on the table with the other Christmas presents. What a surprise, what rejoicing, what celebrations! The money was back where it had come from, only in hands that needed it more this time. In many Belarusian living rooms the recipients drank to the health of their generous benefactor, wishing whoever it was a long and healthy life.

Emma stayed in Mexico for ever. But the good wishes from Belarus must have reached her there. Because some months later she had a baby, a healthy little girl.

The Happy Pork franchise gave Emma an income for the rest of her days.

And when Emma saw pelicans, she knew that Max too had found a new life in a healthy body in a new world.

Without all of you ...

Thanks to all my friends for the ideas, encouragement and criticism they offered me while I was writing this book. Peter Schreiber and Marianne Schönbach, in particular, read many manuscript pages. I would like to thank you both warmly.

Thanks to my parents, who gave me many details about pig breeding.

Thanks to Bettina Woernle, in whose Italian house in San Fiorano I was able to stay quietly writing for weeks.

Thanks to Ilona and Eckhard Dierlich for their information on medical details, and to Waltraut Dennhardt-Herzog for Dagmar's Austrian manner of speech.

I would like to thank Erika Sommer from North Hesse for the story of 'The Calf or the Heart Attack', which she told me years ago.

Warm thanks to my agent Erika Stegmann, who believed firmly in this story.

And special thanks to my editor Maria Koettnitz. She made a manuscript into a book and gave me readers – a writer can ask for nothing better.

The author can be found at: www.schreiber-werkstatt.de